Published in The United States of America
By Pogue Publishing, Beeville, TX

Manufactured in The United States of America
First edition published 2017

This cover is based on a design given to the author by Derek Murphy. Thank you, Derek, for all your help in learning more about cover design.

ISBN: 9781521853931

Wolf's Mission

Lynn Nodima

Dedication

In every author's life, there are people he or she never meets that are none-the-less important to their writing endeavors. This book is dedicated to all those writers who step up to help new writers make their way through the labyrinth of publishing, whether traditionally published or indie published.

Please Leave a Review

Please leave a review letting others know what you thought of this book. Reviews help other readers find books they will enjoy. They are so much appreciated by readers and authors!

Thank you!

Want to Learn More About Lynn Nodima?
Visit her blog at:
www.lynnnodima.com

Chapter 1

Renate Bianchi sat on the cold concrete floor, her back pressed into the corner of the concrete wall, one shoulder resting against each side of the corner. Knees up, arms resting on her knees, and hands dangling between them, she kept her eyes closed, trying to get some rest. With cold silver bars set at five-inch inch intervals meeting the two walls extending from the corner behind her, she was imprisoned in a small equilateral triangular cage, 10 feet to each side.

In the center of the bars, a door also made of silver bars was the only way into or out of the cage. No getting through concrete walls, and no ability to touch the bars long enough to get through them. Renate wasn't sure her werewolf strength would be enough to bend the bars, but the silver kept her from even trying.

In Renate's cage, a flea-infested bed she refused to touch stretched along one wall. A toilet occupied the opposite corner. Only the thin, almost see-through shower curtain taped over a few bars hinted at privacy to use it. On the other side of the bars, two men dressed in black and gray camo trousers and black t-shirts played poker at a folding card table, ignoring her as long as she stayed quiet. Renate didn't recognize the uniforms. They each carried Glock's in holsters under their arms. Not that they needed them. Unless they opened the cage door.

Beyond the two men was another door. She didn't know where it led. She didn't know where she was. Only that she didn't want to be here, and didn't have much choice. She sighed inaudibly. It never occurred to Renate that she was unsafe at a campaign dinner in Washington

D.C.

Someone must have slipped her a roofie. That's the only thing she could figure out. She remembered going to the Ladies Room. The next thing she knew, she woke on that fleabag bed. Fleas would not bite werewolves, but the thought of them crawling on her made her ill. She hated bugs. All bugs. Even the pretty butterflies her mother hatched in her sunroom garden.

When the door beyond the card table opened, Renate strained to hear. Hoping they would believe her sleeping and open the cage door, she felt her muscles tense, ready to move fast if they did. Two, no three, people walked into the room. The two men playing cards scraped their chairs against the concrete floor when they stood up.

"At ease, men."

The voice was new to Renate. Stomping footsteps approached the bars of her cage. "I know you're not sleeping."

Renate considered her options, decided she didn't have any. The 3" polished steel wire hoops she wore in her ears brushed the shoulders of her formal black leather vest as she looked up at the man looking in at her. Her two guards and the other men with him stood at his back. This man was in charge. She could see it in his alpha stance. She almost snickered. Even humans had their alphas. "Why am I here? What do you want?"

The alpha man tilted his head and frowned, his face in the shadow. The single bulb hanging from a cord in the center of the room behind him gave his dirty blonde hair a halo effect. "From you? Nothing. From your father?" His teeth showed ghostly white in the shadow of his face. "Let's just say he has a job to do for us."

Renate glanced at the cage bars. This man knew she was a werewolf. Otherwise, her accommodations would be much less expensive. The silver bars must have cost a fortune. "Dad won't cooperate."

"He will if he wants to see his puppy again."

Chapter 2

Something smelled off. Nate Rollins frowned and glanced at his foster brother, Eli Thomas, as they followed the general into the bowels of a massive military compound. Eli's expression showed he, too, was uncomfortable. Trying to identify what was bothering him, Nate thought back over the last two hours. That the general was unhappy when he found Janelle, Jonathan, and Ben at the helipad was clear. They drove Nate and Eli to the airstrip to wait for the helicopter the general sent for them. The minute Nate and Eli climbed into the chopper, General Brighton put a headset on, started writing something on an electronic tablet, and refused to talk.

He still refused to talk. He marched ahead of them, their steps echoing in the underground corridor, before finally stopping at a metal door. The general pressed his hand to a palm scanner, then led them inside when the door swished open. Behind them, the door swished closed with a finality that had Koreth, Nate's wolf, on edge. Koreth hated being in confined areas even more than Nate did.

The cold, metallic smell of the walls surrounding them felt like an itch he couldn't reach. He hoped he and Eli would be out of the compound and away on their mission soon. They marched down another corridor, then into a small room. In the center of the room, a small table held a block of silver toned metal. Four metal chairs were scooted up beneath the table's edges, one on each side. A combat unit armed with M39s lined the walls, facing the center of the room, their weapons at ready.

Nate's right eyebrow climbed as he took in the rifles

not quite aimed at him and Eli. He turned his attention to the general, waiting for him to speak. General Brighton walked to the opposite side of the table, out of the line of fire, and turned to face Nate and his brother.

The general's piercing gaze studied them, one at a time, then he motioned toward the block of metal on the table. "Pick it up."

Nate frowned. "Sir?"

"Pick it up."

He reached forward. Just before his hand closed on the metal, he felt the itch in his palm increase. Solid silver. As a Royal werewolf, silver didn't affect him much. While it was uncomfortable to his touch, it didn't burn him like it did most werewolves. He swallowed and cast a glance at the general. The general's gaze hardened as Nate hesitated.

He knows about were. Koreth's thought was confirmation of Nate's own. Without further hesitation, he picked up the silver block, bounced it in his hand as if weighing it, tossed it from one hand to the other, then looked at the general again. "What do you want me to do with this, General?"

The general's tension eased a bit, and he shoved his chin toward Eli. "Give it to him."

Nate kept his panic from his expression. *Koreth, can Eli handle silver?* He felt Koreth's affirmation. *He can if we protect him.* Nate looked at Eli. *Koreth, tell Jabril that we will protect him. Tell him to act like it is nothing to handle silver.*

The only indication that Eli received the communication from Jabril, his wolf, was the glance he threw at Nate. Without hesitation, Eli lifted the metal from Nate's hand and turned it in his hand. His expression curious, Eli set it on the table and looked at the general. "What's up, General?"

"Hold out your hands, palm up."

Nate and Eli extended their arms, showing the general their unburned palms. The general sighed and nodded toward the chairs. "Sit down, men." He turned to the combat unit. "Dismissed."

Nate and Eli sat and waited until the soldiers left the room, closing the door behind them. The general sat and faced them. "Sorry about that. After finding you on the ranch, I had to know for sure."

Nate's eyes narrowed. "Know what for sure, Sir?"

General Brighton chuckled. "You'll think I'm crazy, but the truth is, I needed to know if you'd been turned."

"Turned?" Nate ignored the tension rolling off Eli. "You know we're loyal."

"I knew you were loyal, but things can change if a man turns."

Nate studied the general. He schooled his expression into one of confusion. "How would a block of metal tell you we weren't loyal?"

"I needed to know if you are werewolves."

Nate laughed. "Werewolves? There are such things as werewolves?" Inside, he wasn't laughing at all. He shrugged. "Okay, then, if there really are werewolves, how about you pick up the metal. Just so we know you're human."

The general looked at the block of silver and shook his head. "I can't. It would burn me."

Chapter 3

Nate caught his breath. He didn't have to try to display the shock he felt, it covered his face. The general smelled strange, but he didn't smell of werewolf. "You're a werewolf?"

A stubborn, defensive attitude radiated from the general. "I am not a werewolf." He shrugged and sighed. "Unfortunately, I share the same weakness to silver as werewolves. It is, however, on a need to know. And you don't need to know."

Nate and Eli exchanged glances. Nate turned back to the general and nodded. "Fair enough. I can understand need to know." He leaned forward. "What I don't understand is why being on the ranch made you think we might be werewolves."

When he realized the general was going to brush off his question, Nate crossed his arms and settled into his chair. "That *is* need to know, General. I need to know."

"Tell me why you were on the ranch and I'll consider answering your question."

Impasse. Nate kept his face blank and stared at his commanding officer. "The people on that ranch are family and friends."

"Family. You said that before."

Nate nodded. "They will be soon. I'm getting married."

The general looked startled. For a moment, Nate thought he was going to call the combat squad back. When Nate just blinked and watched him, though, the general calmed down. General Brighton looked from Nate to Eli. "You getting married, too?"

"No, Sir. I just work there."

"Doing?"

"I'm helping build some houses."

"Houses." General Brighton glared at Eli. "Son, if you lie to me..."

"He's helping build houses. I asked him to."

The general's eyes turned to Nate. "Why would you do that?"

Nate shrugged. "We needed a few more houses. Why do you care?"

"I could have you incarcerated as traitors. You wouldn't even get a trial."

Nate sucked his teeth and nodded. "I know that. This whole team is need to know only. Far as I know, the president doesn't even know about us."

"So, why don't you make this easier on yourselves and answer my questions?"

With a glance at Eli, Nate shrugged. "Let's just say I'm curious. Since you seem to think you need to know, my fiancé's brother and his family recently died. She needed help with the ranch, so I took the job of ranch manager."

"Kind of out of your wheelhouse, isn't it?"

Nate grinned. "Pays better than being a cop."

The general scratched his nose and frowned. "Randal Hynson's dead?"

Right eyebrow raised, Nate studied the general. "You knew Hynson?"

"We met. How did he die?"

"He was murdered." Nate leaned forward. "How did you know him?"

"Do you know who killed him?"

"Someone named Lorena Black and her family."

General Brighton's eyes bored into Nate's as if he could force Nate to tell him what he wanted to know. Nate returned the look for several seconds and was surprised when Koreth forced him to look down at the table. *What?*

Koreth's growl filled Nate's mind. *Vampire! Don't look into his eyes.*

Nate blinked. *Tell Jabril.* He let out a loud sigh. "Look, General, I think there's something you're not telling me, but I also figure if I need to know, you'll say so." Clearing his throat, he shrugged. "Why not tell us why you called? Eli said it has something to do with a special agent being missing." Nate looked up at the general but focused on his nose.

General Brighton frowned at him. "If you weren't the only two men in the squad who could do this, I'd bust you down to private."

"Do what?"

"Retrieve the agent. The cage she's being held in has silver-lined bars. Otherwise, she could get herself out of there."

Nate's left thumb started thumping against the table. When Eli cleared his throat and looked pointedly at his hand, Nate frowned and pressed his hand flat on the table. "So, if she can't get out of a silver-lined cage, she must be, what, a werewolf?"

For a moment, he thought the general would refuse to answer. "Need to know, General." Nate's gaze side-swiped Eli then returned to the general. "Don't want her biting my brother, you know."

Eli huffed and muttered, "As if."

Nate snickered but his kept gaze on Brighton. He didn't intend to go Lycos on the general, but if he had to, he would. And if he did, he wondered if the general would react the same way the *were* pack had. Lycos was the ruler of all *were*, vampires, and more. The general didn't know who he was dealing with. And if Nate had his way, he never would.

Another thought occurred to him. "If no one else on the squad can go after her, what are they? They werewolves, too?"

The general pursed his lips. He glared at Nate.

Nate rested his elbows on the table and clasped his right hand in his left. "You're telling me that, even though we've been a part of this squad for years, you've been hiding something that big from us?"

"You didn't need to know."

"And now."

The general's chair scraped concrete. He stood and paced across the room several times, then stopped at the table and leaned on it, both hands flat on the surface. "Suppose let's stop this dance, Colonel." He looked at Eli and then back at Nate. "What do you want to know?"

"Are all the members of the team werewolves?"

"No."

When the general didn't elaborate, Nate wiped his chin with his large hand. "Then what are they?"

No answer.

Nate stood up, copied the general's stance, both hands flat on the table. "You've never had cause to distrust us before. Why now?"

"Things have changed."

"Changed how?"

"Wait here." A moment later, the large metal door swished shut behind the general, closing with a clang.

Eli frowned. "Think we can get out if he decides to keep us locked up?"

Nate ran his hand through his hair and shrugged. "Hopefully, we won't have to find out." *Koreth tell Jabril to let Eli know they've got cameras and mics on us.*

Eli blinked but otherwise didn't show any response. Nate sat back down, crossed his arms over his chest and tipped his chair back. He pulled his cap down over his eyes. "Be nice to have a rest."

"A rest." Through the tight mesh fabric of his cap, Nate saw Eli shake his head. "I think Janelle's been working you too hard."

Nate shrugged. "She's a hard taskmaster. Wants those houses up last week."

"Yeah."

"Shut up for a while. If we have to stay here, I might as well get that nap I missed."

Nate grinned at Eli's muttered curse. His eyes never closed, but those on the other side of the camera couldn't see that with his cap on his face. *Koreth, see what you can sense.*

Koreth stretched his senses, listening for thoughts and smelling for *were* traces. After several minutes, Koreth turned his attention back to Nate. *Seven werewolves, five werebears, three werelions, four vampires. The troops are all human, and don't know about the were or vampires. The vamps have them under compulsion not to notice anything they would consider strange.*

Under the cap, Nate blinked. *Werelions*?

He felt Koreth's amusement. *You accept werewolves, werepanthers, werebears, and vampires, but balk at werelions?*

The door opened again. Nate's chair crashed forward, upright in the correct position. He pulled his cap from his face. When he saw who entered, Nate surged to his feet, saluting Secretary Bianchi, Secretary of Defense. A moment later, he felt Eli jerk to attention next to him.

Bianchi studied them for a moment, then returned their salutes. "At ease, men. Have a chair."

"Sir, yes, Sir!" Nate and Eli dropped into their chairs. Koreth sniffed. *Werewolf.*

Bianchi moved closer to them, sniffing. He turned to look at Brighton. "They don't smell *were.*"

"No, Sir."

"But you want to tell them, anyway."

Brighton swallowed. "Without the intel, they don't have a chance for success."

"You trust them."

"Always have."

Bianchi raised an eyebrow. "And now?"

Brighton looked a Nate and Eli, then sighed. "There's something different about them, but they're the same obnoxious leathernecks they always were."

Bianchi turned to Nate. "Can we trust you, soldier?"

"With your life, Sir."

"Let's hope it doesn't come to that." Bianchi rubbed his neck, glanced at Brighton, then nodded. "Alright. As long as they understand the restrictions and agree to abide by them."

"Thank you, Sir." Brighton looked relieved. "I believe they are Renate's best chance for survival."

Nate blinked. *Renate Bianchi? The Secretary's daughter?* "Sir, is Miss Bianchi in trouble?"

"She's been captured by terrorists who think they can force me to...let's just say, perform a specific action for them."

"What kind of action, Sir?"

Nate thought the secretary was going to ignore the question, then he sighed and motioned at Brighton to shut the door. "They want me to assassinate the president."

"Or..."

Bianchi cursed. "They'll kill her. After torture, of course."

Nate stared at the secretary's eyes. *He speaks truth.* Nate nodded. *Thanks, Koreth. Will he do it, if we can't get to her?*

He felt Koreth's displeasure. *He will.*

Nate sighed. *Guess I can't blame him. If it was Janelle...* "We'll go get her and bring her back, Secretary." He scratched his forehead and looked at Eli, making sure he got Koreth's message, too.

Eli nodded and asked, "Just what is it that we need to know that seems to get everyone's tighty whities tighter?"

"She's a werewolf."

Nate nodded. "We already figured that out. That means you are a werewolf, too." Nate studied the narrowing of the secretary's eyes. "Why can't you go after her?"

"I can't get her out of a silver-lined cage. Otherwise, she would already be home."

"Uh huh. How long do we have before…?"

"Their deadline for the President's demise is three days from now."

Nate whistled. "Not much time, then. She part of the squad?"

The secretary glanced at Brighton, then looked at Nate. "You ask a lot of questions for someone who walked away."

"You need us, Secretary. We need to know. How well trained is she? When we get her out of the cage, is she going to be a delicate daffodil, or can she fight?"

"You get her out, and the men who put her there will

probably not live to notify their employers of her escape."

"So, she's a trained agent. How will she know to trust us?" He grinned at Bianchi. "Don't want to have to tie her up to keep from getting hurt, you understand."

When the secretary scowled at him, Nate's grin widened. Finally, the secretary nodded. He reached into his pocket and pulled out a medallion like the four melded medallions hidden beneath Nate's shirt. Involuntarily, Nate took a step back, knocking his chair to the floor.

The secretary's sharp gaze raked him. "You know what this is?"

"There was one on the ranch." Nate cursed himself. He hadn't intended to say that.

Bianchi reached out his hand toward Nate, the medallion in it. Nate watched it move closer with as much dread as most would if a poisonous snake stretched out toward them. After the Ancients put him on trial for having four, he wasn't about to touch the fifth and final medallion. He wasn't sure he would survive it.

Before it reached Nate, Eli leaned forward and grabbed it, careful, Nate noted, to catch the chain rather than the pendant. He held it up and let the medallion twist in the air. "What an interesting medallion. Is it a family heirloom?"

Secretary Bianchi frowned. "Yes. She will know it."

Eli pulled a clean bandana from his pocket and carefully wrapped the medallion and chain, then slipped it into his pocket. "We'll get it to her, Secretary." Eli grinned at Bianchi as if he hadn't a care in the world. "When do we leave?"

Nate swallowed, briefly closed his eyes, and cautiously let out a soft breath of relief. He nodded and gave Bianchi a weak smile when the secretary glanced at him. "We'll get her back, Sir."

Chapter 4

Nate was thankful for Eli's quick action in taking the medallion from the secretary. He could still feel the pull of it, even with it in Eli's pocket. As much as he dreaded the thought of touching the medallion, his fingers twitched for it. *You are forbidden.* Nate nodded, knowing Koreth was right. Taking the medallion would mean another trial, one he would not likely survive.

"Under no circumstance will you put the medallion chain around your neck." Bianchi's voice was harsh, threatening.

"Of course not, Sir," answered Eli with a shrug. "It's not mine."

Bianchi glared at Eli for a long breath, then harrumphed. "Don't forget it."

"No, Sir." Eli kept his face blank while returning the secretary's stare.

Nate cleared his throat. "Who has Renate, Sir? And where?"

The secretary sighed and motioned toward the chairs. "Sit down."

Nate stood his chair upright and sat; Eli sat in the chair beside him. Bianchi and the general also sat at the table, then the secretary leaned toward Nate. "She was at a political dinner in Washington D.C. Terrorists calling themselves the Black Forest Huntsmen kidnapped her. We've tracked them to British Columbia, at an old factory that shut down over twenty years ago."

Nate leaned his elbows on the table, right hand folded in his left hand. "Black Forest Huntsmen? Werewolves?"

"No, they're human. The Black Forest Huntsmen are an Old-World group, originally from Germany. *Were* hunters. In centuries past, they hunted werewolves almost to extinction. More recently, they've added other *were* to their list of targets." He stopped at Nate's frown. "Having trouble believing all this, Colonel?"

Nate shook his head. "Just wondering why they didn't kill her, instead of capturing her."

"In the past fifty years or so, the Huntsmen have been striving to infiltrate the world's major governments. That is easier to do when there is confusion." The secretary glanced at General Brighton and sighed. "Killing the president would cause the kind of confusion they're after."

"So, there's someone in place to step in and cause more trouble?"

Bianchi nodded. "The president is unaware of *were*. However, the vice president is a member of the Huntsmen. Has been since his twenties. He won't assassinate the president. He won't take the risk the Secret Service will stop him. And thereby put a stop to their plans."

"But as a trusted member of the presidential staff, you could get close enough to have it done before the Secret Service could react."

The general nodded at Nate's assessment. "Right. And since he's *were*, Secretary Bianchi could get away. Unless they have silver bullets or know to try for a head shot. If Secretary Bianchi kills him, they achieve two goals. Chaos allowing the vice president to step into the president's office. As the new president, he could create new laws against *were* using executive orders. The president's death would expose *were* to the general population, causing fear. Average citizens would take up the anti-*were* position, and *were* would be hunted again."

Bianchi shuddered. "If that happens, a lot of innocent humans will die, as well as innocent *were*." He stared at his clenched hands. "I can't let that happen."

Nate frowned at the secretary's white knuckles. "Nor can we, Secretary. We'll get her out. Alive. And we'll do anything we can to stop them."

The finality in Nate's tone seemed to surprise both the general and the secretary. Nate crossed his arms and leaned on the table, his left thumb beating a fast tempo against the tabletop. For a moment, he closed his eyes, thinking, then he looked at Eli. Eli raised an eyebrow at him but didn't comment.

Nate stood and paced the small room, trying to decide how much to tell his two superiors. He stopped, facing the blank gray wall, and stood in thought for several seconds before pivoting on his heel to face the table. After blowing out a long breath, he crossed the room and sat down.

"There's something I want to tell you."

The general exchanged glances with the secretary. Both men were suddenly on edge as if they dreaded what he might say. "What's that?" the general finally asked.

"I already knew about werewolves." Nate licked his lips. "We both did."

No one moved. Bianchi finally nodded. "Someone at the ranch tell you?"

Nate looked at Eli, eyebrow raised. Eli hesitated, then nodded his agreement. Nate turned back to Bianchi. "I'm a werewolf, too."

Bianchi frowned. "You don't smell *were*."

"No, I don't."

"And that's because?"

Nate bit his lip. *In for a penny...* Hearing the cliché in his foster-mother's voice in his mind, he almost grinned. Instead, he reached inside his shirt and pulled out the melded medallion he wore. "My medallion prevents detection by other *were*."

Both men gawked at the medallion in Nate's hand, then the secretary put his hand out. "I'll be taking that."

"No, you won't."

"That wasn't a suggestion. It was an order."

"That's just it, secretary. I can't remove it. It's not that I won't, but I can't." Nate sighed. "It only comes off if I die."

"That could be arranged."

Nate knew Bianchi's threat was serious. Knew Bianchi intended to have the medallion. He laughed. "You can try."

Bianchi frowned. "What makes you think I can't?"

"You had one. You ever wear it?"

The Secretary studied Nate's face and shook his head. "It was passed down from my grandfather. Wearing it was forbidden."

"There's a reason for that."

"Oh? And that reason is?"

"Nate, I don't think..."

Chopping his hand in the air to silence Eli, Nate considered the two men in front of him. "It changes you. Makes you different. Not who you are, or what you think and believe, but what you are." Nate leaned forward. "And the rest is need to know, gentlemen. You don't need to know."

There was a dangerous glint in Bianchi's eyes. "Where did you get it?"

"It was my dad's. He gave it to me before he died, over

twenty years ago."

Brighton and Bianchi exchanged glances again, then the general jerked his chin toward Eli. "And him? He a werewolf, too?"

Eli answered before Nate could. "I am."

"You wearing a medallion, too?" asked Bianchi.

"No, Sir. I don't have one."

"Then how could either of you handle silver? And why can't I smell *were* on you?"

Eli blinked, startled. He frowned and looked at Nate. Ignoring the first question, Eli zeroed in on the second. "Why can't he smell *were* on me, Nate?"

Nate shrugged. "I don't know unless it's because you've been my brother, friend, and partner for so long." He rubbed the back of his neck. "Or maybe because my blood turned you."

Bianchi narrowed his eyes at Eli. "You were human?"

"Yeah." Eli gave him a sheepish grin. "We did the blood brother thing when we were just stupid kids. Didn't know any better."

A loud tap sounded at the door. Annoyance obvious, Brighton walked to the door and opened it. He stepped out, then after a pause shut the door behind him. Nate and Eli had time to exchange glances before the door opened again. The same combat unit that had occupied the room earlier marched in, rifles aimed at Nate and Eli. Nate tilted his head and frowned at the General.

The secretary jumped to his feet and moved out of the line of fire. "What's going on, General?"

General Brighton studied Nate for a moment. "Just so you know, these rifles are loaded with silver bullets. Want to tell me about the Were Council, Nate?"

Sighing, Nate shrugged. "Not much to tell."

"Reports say you killed Jackson."

"Do your reports also say he was planning to kill more than 40 innocents?"

"Explain, and make it good."

Nate noticed the anxious look in Eli's face. *Koreth, tell Jabril we can stop the bullets if they fire.* Eli swallowed but nodded his understanding. Nate leaned back in his chair, arms crossed over his chest. "Queen Lenora and her family of Toms attacked the ranch, killing all but a few of the wolves. They used poison to incapacitate them long enough to rip their hearts out. Even the children."

Nate stopped briefly when Bianchi gasped, then continued. "During subsequent fights, Lenora and her three toms were killed. When the wolf pack reported the deaths to the Were Council, as Council law required, the Council passed a death sentence on the entire clowder. Innocent men, women, and children."

Nate looked at the table for a moment, remembering the fight with Jackson. "As Alpha to the wolf pack, I accepted the new Queen's request for sanctuary and adopted the clowder into the pack." He looked up and almost grinned at the shock on the secretary's face.

"You are the pack Alpha?" The secretary sounded as if he was strangling.

With a nod, Nate said, "I refused to allow the Council to kill innocents. They showed up. Jackson wanted me dead, and used their adoption as an excuse to condemn the pack as well as the clowder."

Nate shrugged. "He challenged. We fought. I won. He died. It's as simple as that."

The secretary's face paled. "So, you are Council Alpha,

as well."

"That's what they tell me. I got the call from the general before I could really determine what all that involves."

Abruptly standing, the secretary paced the room. Nate watched, impassive. After his third time across the room, the secretary spun and faced Nate. "I have ways of checking up on what you said. If you've lied to me..."

Again, Nate shrugged. "I haven't, but either way, you need us."

Chapter 5

Six hours after Nate and Eli flew away in the helicopter, Janelle Hynson sat at the kitchen bar with Flora Garrett, sipping coffee. Janelle studied the rose pattern on her mug and sighed. Six hours, and she already missed Nate. She cupped her left hand protectively over her belly and hoped he would return in time for the baby's birth. Flora's sympathetic silence helped settle her nerves.

Janelle looked up and sighed. "Maybe we should work on getting the school set up."

"You have a place for a school?"

Memories of the children slain by the old queen tried to crowd Janelle's mind. She shuddered and pushed them away. "I think we need to have a different school house. I don't think the wolf kids could study there, now."

"Oh?"

"The children were in school when they were killed. The wolf kids still alive helped with their funeral."

"I am so sorry, Janelle."

For a moment, Janelle was lost in thought, then felt misery flooding her friend. She had always been perceptive to other's emotions, but since her pregnancy, she hadn't been able to block them. Janelle caught Flora's hand in her own and squeezed. "It's not your fault, Flora. You would have stopped her if you had known."

Flora nodded. "I am thankful you know that."

Janelle smiled at her. "I have an idea. How about we ask the construction team to build a small school house between the picnic shelter and the warehouse, a classroom for the preschool and kinder classes, one for the younger kids, and one for the teens? As needed, we can add more rooms." Janelle was rewarded by the excited look on Flora's face.

"That's perfect! We'll have them make the rooms large, with sliding panels that can easily divide them into six rooms, when needed. That way, it will be a while before we need more classrooms. Jonathan can teach the teens, and I'll teach the middles. Councilman Bradley's wife can teach the preschool and kindergarten kids." Flora looked puzzled. "What was her name, again?"

Janelle thought for a moment and shrugged. "I don't think he mentioned it. Jonathan probably knows. She should be here early next week." She slipped off her stool and carried her cup to the coffee pot. After pouring herself another cup, she quirked an eyebrow at Flora. "Refill?"

"What? Oh. No, thanks. Too much caffeine makes me jittery."

Janelle set the pot down, moved back to her stool, and gazed through the window at the teens working out with Ben and Dusty. Tig ran circles around the group, barking at them. When Eli first brought Tig to the ranch, she worried he might not get along with the wolves and panthers. For some reason, the golden Labrador took to Dusty and preferred his company over that of others. Dusty took over the dog's care, and Tig followed him everywhere.

She grinned when Adrian and Reese pulled monkey faces behind Ben's and Dusty's backs, then laughed when Dusty ordered them to run the compound for their shenanigans. Those two finally put their differences aside and became fast friends. Janelle hoped the other kids would follow their lead. Still grinning, she turned her attention to the Clowder Queen.

Flora's clasped hands were resting on the kitchen bar, and she was staring at them. "We'll need a teacher's workroom, and maybe an office, too. What kind of budget do we have for the school and supplies?"

"Pretty much whatever we need, we can have. Get me a list of supplies, and I'll get it all ordered." Janelle bit her lip, then asked, "Did you ever hear of *were* getting married like humans?"

Flora looked up at Janelle and laughed. "No." After seeing Janelle's face, she sobered. "Why?"

"You know Nate was raised by humans?"

"Yeah?"

"He wants to have a big wedding, right here on the ranch, and invite his human family and friends."

Flora blew out a loud breath. "Is that a good idea?"

With a shrug, Janelle grinned. "I don't know, but he told me to plan it while he's gone. He wants to get married in the two-story gazebo." She sucked her bottom lip between her teeth, then said in a rush, "I don't know how to plan a human wedding. Will you help me?"

Flora grinned. "I've never planned a wedding, either." She gave Janelle a tight hug. "I think it's great! You know, with this example, there may be more weddings in our pack future." She looked wistful for a moment, and Janelle realized she was thinking of Will. Then Flora leaned back and smiled. "What do you want me to do?"

Janelle swallowed, then laughed. "I guess I need a cake and a dress. At least, that's what I've seen on television. They have bridesmaids, too, but all my wolf friends..." She bowed her head for a minute, then pushed her grief away. "Would you be my maid of honor?"

Flora's eyes danced at the thought. "I would be happy

to be your maid of honor. Thank you."

"Maybe we should check the Internet and see what else we need."

"Good idea! Let's go." Flora took Janelle's hand and pulled her off the stool.

Laughing, Janelle allowed her friend to lead her down the hall to the stairs. Together, they raced to the office to get Janelle's school laptop and start their research on all things bridal.

Chapter 6

Raw meat slapped the cold concrete floor just inches in front of Renate's feet, splattering blood on her black slacks. She tilted her head back to look at the sepia-skinned man sneering at her. After a quick glance at his partner, laughing from his seat at the table, Renate pursed her lips tight and gave the first a blank stare.

"I'm not eating that."

"Suit yourself." He shrugged. "The dogs like it."

She let *were* touch her eyes, making them briefly glow. He shuddered and swallowed. Her gaze trapped him. She had the power to freeze him as long as she kept her gaze on him, but compulsion was beyond her. Unfortunately, that was a vampire trait. While a few very powerful werewolves had it, she wasn't one of them. Otherwise, he would have already opened her cage for her.

She raised one corner of her mouth in a mirthless smirk. *It scares him for you to look at him like that.* Renate agreed with Salena, her wolf. But if she found a way to get out of the cage, it wouldn't be the way she looked at him that he needed to worry about.

The door behind him shoved open. The man she designated as alpha man walked in. She glanced at alpha man, releasing the guard. The man in front of her spun around and snapped to attention, inadvertently moving a few inches closer to the bars. Pursing her lips, she considered grabbing him from behind. He probably didn't have the keys to the cell in his pockets, but it would almost be worth the burns to find out. A chuckle brought her gaze to alpha man.

"I wouldn't stand so close to those bars if I was you."

"Sir?"

"You're close enough that she can reach you. And your gun." His gaze turned to her. "From the looks of her, I don't think a few silver burns would keep her from breaking your neck."

Renate laughed aloud when the man previously tormenting her gasped and jumped away from the cage. He whipped around, staring at her as she shook her head, and focused on alpha man. "Your people aren't trained very well."

Frowning at her, alpha man crossed his arms and studied her. Renate shrugged. She still sat on the floor leaning into the corner. Shifting her legs to sit cross-legged, she leaned forward and waved her hand at the raw meat on the floor in front of her. "Nor do they have manners. A girl has preferences how her steak is served." She smirked at him. "After all, I'm not an animal."

His harsh laugh sent shivers down her spine. "But that's exactly what you are, wolf. An animal."

"Said the animal that locked me in a cage."

Eyes hard, he stopped laughing. "Just thought you would like to know your father has agreed to our terms. To obtain your release, the president's assassination will be broadcast on all news channels by midnight tomorrow."

Renate froze but forced her expression not to change. "I don't believe you."

"You don't have to. You'll see it for yourself when we release you." He gave her an evil grin and snapped his fingers. "Oh, that's right. You won't. We will return you to him, but you won't be alive."

"I assumed as much."

"Did you?" He laughed. "Figured out who we are, did you?"

"Huntsmen."

"Not bad. What gave it away?"

Renate shrugged. "The stench in here is getting worse all the time."

The laughter on his face vanished. "You die at dawn after the president dies." With that, he spun on his heel and marched out.

At least now, she knew how long she had to figure something out. Renate studied the door he slammed, then looked at the two men on the other side of the bars. She let her eyes glow *were*, then smiled and tilted her head. Leaning forward, she picked up the raw meat in front of her and threw it through the bars to the center of their card table, splattering blood on the cards. "I won't be needing this, boys. I prefer my meals live."

Both jumped when she let her wolf out enough to growl at them. They moved their chairs to the opposite wall and turned to face her before sitting. The bitter smell of fear wafted from them, and Renate laughed. "Night, boys."

Leaning her head back against the corner behind her, she shut her eyes. She prayed her father had a plan to get her out. If not, she would need to be rested when they came for her. Renate didn't doubt alpha man would try to kill her. She didn't even doubt that he might be able to do it. But she wouldn't die alone.

Chapter 7

Six hours later, with one layover for refueling, Nate and Eli picked up the duffle the general provided each of them and deplaned the UC-35C in Seattle, Washington. As the only passengers, they had been able to get some sleep. When they stepped off the plane, a Jeep pulled up in front of them. The soldier wearing regulation trousers and an olive-green t-shirt jumped out and snapped a salute. "I'm Corporal Donald Dunn, Sir, your driver and assistant while you are here."

Nate and Eli returned the salute, stowed their bags in the back of the Jeep, and climbed into the Jeep, Nate sitting in the front. Corporal Dunn slid behind the wheel. Nate glanced at Dunn. "Based in Bangor, Corporal?"

"Yes, Sir." Corporal Dunn glanced at Nate. "I have motel rooms rented."

A half-hour later, Dunn pulled into a small chain motel. Nate and Eli jumped out of the Jeep, Corporal Dunn looked at them, waiting for orders. "Corporal, we'll need something less conspicuous to drive around in than a military Jeep, and you will need to be dressed in civvies. Casual. Jeans and a different t-shirt would be fine."

"Yes, Sir. If you wish, I could request a rental from the base."

Nate scratched his whiskers, annoyed that he hadn't had time for a shave today and nodded. "That works." He pulled his duffel out of the Jeep. "Let's toss our gear in our rooms and get a bite to eat." He raised an eyebrow at the corporal. "Have you had time to eat supper, Corporal?"

"No, Sir."

"You're with us, then."

After depositing their duffels in their rooms, Nate started walking toward the burger joint across the highway from the motel. "Mind if I use your first name, Corporal?"

"No, Sir."

"Donald, I'm Nate and this..." He waved his hand toward his brother. "…is Eli. While we're here, we are the best of friends. Don't call either of us sir."

"Yes, Si...Nate."

Nate grinned at his slip. "It might mean our lives, Donald. Your friends call you Donald or Don?"

"Don."

Nate nodded with approval. "Okay, Don. Let's get a burger, then we'll contact the general." He stopped to allow a car to pull into the drive-through lane, then walked to the restaurant door. "You staying at the same motel, Don?"

"Yes. We have a block of three rooms, all together."

Nate grinned when Don caught himself before adding 'sir.' "I know it's not regulation, Don, but this whole operation is unconventional. And life or death. For more than one person."

Don blinked but didn't seem to be surprised. "The general told me it might be dangerous."

An hour later, the men gathered in Nate's room. Nate took the last sip of his soda and tossed the cup into the motel room trash can. Nate sat in the only chair, and the other two sat side-by-side on the closest bed. After hearing Nate's plans to cross into Canada, Don frowned.

"Sir, I mean, Nate, do we have permission to cross into Canada for a military mission?"

"We do not. As far as anyone will know, we are going for a pleasure trip. This mission is need-to-know only. We'll drive up to British Columbia, take care of business, and come back."

"May I ask what we're supposed to do there?"

Nate exchanged glances with Eli, then looked back at Don. "What's your training, Corporal?"

"Force Recon, Sir."

At least the general sent someone who might make it out alive. "We are going to rescue the daughter of a member of the president's cabinet. She's been kidnapped. They're using her to force her father to commit treason. His deadline is midnight tomorrow. We're going to get her out before then." He took a deep breath, then leaned forward. "Eli and I are going after her. You will be doing touristy type things, visiting the planetarium and museums, or whatever you want to do."

"You won't need my help?"

"We'll split up as soon as we're over the border. If she is able, she'll join us on the return trip. If not, I'll think of something."

The corporal didn't look happy. Nate raised his eyebrow. "Problem?"

"My orders are to stay with you, Sir. As backup."

"Or a watchdog." Nate grinned at Don's stoic expression. "I should have realized the general was still not sure of us." His shoulders hitched up in a shrug. "Orders are orders, I suppose. Just don't get in the way."

Don's eyes narrowed. "I'll keep that in mind, Sir."

"Nate..."

Chopping his hand through the air, Nate cut off Eli's protest. "What do you know about paranormal beings, Corporal?"

"Sir?"

"Paranormal beings. You know, genies, vampires, witches, werewolves... What do you know about them?"

The first sign of anger touched the corporal's eyes. Don opened his mouth to answer, but Nate raised his left hand, palm out, to stop him before he spoke. "That's what I thought. Get the general on the phone."

Chapter 8

Janelle frowned at the former councilman standing in her path. With Nate gone, she was in charge of the pack. A concept Bradley didn't seem to understand. Sweltering in the mid-afternoon Texas heat, she frowned. She had too much to do today to spend time listening to his complaints. Again. His belligerent tone grated against her nerves. Especially when the heat was already getting to her. She couldn't remember it being so miserable and wondered if it was due to being pregnant. Bradley waved his hand, snagging her attention.

"You just don't know what you are doing," he insisted. "The bears are not trustworthy."

Sighing, Janelle looked past Bradley. Dusty and Ben had noticed Bradley's threatening stance and were running toward her, Tig on their heels. "The bears have been pardoned. They are welcome here. You, on the other hand, have not been pardoned. If Nate didn't want to keep tabs on you, you would not be welcome here."

Bradley raised to his full height, trying to intimidate her. "Listen, you little she-wolf..."

Dusty grabbed him from behind and threw him to the ground. "When you speak to your Queen, speak respectfully!"

Snarling, Bradley jumped to his feet. "I do not accept her as my Queen. She's nothing but..."

Dusty's fist slammed him in the mouth. Again, the former councilman hit the dirt. Before Dusty could shift and finish him, Janelle touched his arm. Bowing, Dusty stepped back to let her take over. She was aware that he was ready to step in if Bradley persisted.

"That's enough." Janelle spoke to Bradley rather than Dusty. She ignored the blood dripping from his nose to his chin. "Until the supper meal, you will confine yourself to the picnic shelter." He angrily swiped at the blood on his face and started to argue, but Nadrai, her wolf, cast compulsion on him. Until Nadrai allowed, he would not be able to speak.

Janelle let her wolf shine in her eyes. "I've had just about enough of you. Nate sentenced you to live on the ranch and work as a helper to the bears in their construction." She leaned toward him, menace in both her tone and stance. "I have the authority to change that sentence. After all you have done, it won't take much for me to do that."

Stupid wolf that he was, he glared at her. Janelle huffed out her exasperation. "Shelter. Now. And do not move from there until time for the evening meal."

She watched him march stiff-legged to the shelter and knew he was fighting the compulsion with all his ability. Shaking her head, she smiled at Dusty and Ben. "Thank you. Both of you."

Ben scratched the top of his not-so-balding head. "You could have handled him. We just wanted him to know we backed you in whatever you said."

Janelle laughed. "I appreciate that." She studied the top of Ben's head for a moment. "Mind if I ask you something, Ben?"

"What's that?"

"You were gray-haired and almost bald when you got here a few weeks ago. Now, your hair is dark and the bald is nearly gone. What happened?"

An embarrassed grin touched his lips. His hand dropped from his head. "I spent 35 years in the same job, working with humans. Couldn't let them see I don't age the same as they do. I've been using peroxide to lighten my hair and shaving a bald spot onto the top of my head for years." He shrugged. "Just didn't seem to be an issue here, so I stopped."

Janelle grinned, then laughed out loud when Dusty snickered. "Well, it looks nice." She nodded across the compound to a couple of werepanther women walking toward them. "I think Dottie likes it."

Ben turned to look in the direction Janelle indicated. Janelle sucked her lips between her teeth when she saw his eyes widen and his face pale as he identified Dottie and Flora, his daughter. Swallowing, he looked back at Janelle and gave her a quick nod. "Since you don't need help, I'll get back to the kids."

Janelle covered her mouth with her hand, trying to control her mirth as she watched him practically run back to the group of teens he was training. Dusty snickered again, and Janelle glanced at him. "He really likes Dottie, doesn't he?" she asked.

Dusty's gravel voice was the result of being chained in a silver collar for decades. "Yeah, but he won't admit it. Not even to himself."

Turning to face Dusty, Janelle tilted her head and quirked an eyebrow. "And who do you like?"

Dusty matched her quirked eyebrow with one of his own. "What makes you think I like someone?"

"Just hoping, I suppose. After all you've been through, you deserve some happiness." She frowned when his face smoothed into an expressionless mask. She raised her hand toward him. "Dusty..."

He stepped back, avoiding her touch, and gave her a stiff bow. "I must get back to work, my Queen."

Before she could answer, he marched toward Ben and the teens. Janelle watched him go. *I wish...* She felt Nadrai's compassion. *Yes, but he is too damaged to think of finding someone, yet.* Janelle blinked away tears, unwilling to let the approaching women see them. "If Nate hadn't killed Jackson," she whispered to her wolf, "I would be tempted to do it myself." Again, she felt Nadrai's agreement. *Dusty will heal. We must give him time.*

Janelle sighed, frowning at the shudder that coursed through her. Forgetting the torture Nate's uncle, Jackson, put Dusty through was not easy when he carried the scars of silver-burn on his neck and wrists for everyone to see. His courage to bear those scars in full sight rather than try to hide them amazed her.

As Dottie and Flora reached her, Janelle turned her mind to other matters. With a smile, she nodded to them. "Do you have a list of supplies we need for the school?"

She noted Flora's curious glance toward the shelter where Bradley sat, his face set in stubborn defiance, and was relieved when Flora turned back, ignoring him. "I think Dottie has most of it taken care of. If you have time, we could go over it and see if there's anything else you think we should add."

Dottie nodded toward the clipboard she carried. "This list encompasses everything we've used in schools before, but..." She gave Janelle a wry grin. "...we've never had wolf kids in our school, so there might be something we missed."

Janelle grinned. "As Nate is fond of reminding me, Dottie, kids are kids, regardless of parentage." She nodded toward the house. "Let's get out of this heat and have a glass of tea while we look it over."

Flora and Dottie happily agreed. They turned toward the house, and Janelle cast a quick glance at Bradley. *He's going to cause trouble.* Nadrai's growl concurred with Janelle's assessment.

Chapter 9

Eli paced Nate's room. Nate had taken his call with the general outside to the center of the huge parking lot. A quick glance out the window told him Nate was still standing in the same spot, talking with the general. Their mission was dicey enough without having to worry about someone else. Nate, as usual, was annoyed when things happened he had no control over. Eli didn't blame him. Don stood at the window, watching Nate. When Don turned to face him, Eli's right eyebrow climbed. "Question, Don?"

Don jerked his head toward the window. "He always so uptight?"

"Keeps him alive." Eli ignored the studied look Don gave him.

"Uh huh." Don frowned. "He serious about the paranormal stuff?"

Eli sighed and rolled his shoulders. The tension was giving him a headache. He pinched the bridge of his nose between his eyes. "You'll have to ask Nate." Frowning, Eli looked up to see Don's piercing blue eyes focused squarely on him. He wasn't sure what Don was going to say, but the man snapped his mouth shut when the motel room door opened. Peripherally, he noticed that Don turned with him to see Nate walk in.

"What did he say?"

Ignoring Don, an annoyed look on his face, Nate shook his head at Eli. "General wants us to take him with us."

"He knows we can't promise he won't find out?"

"He knows." Nate sighed and looked at Don. "Sorry, soldier. I know you're good, or you wouldn't be a Raider. It's just that this is outside the usual mission scope."

"How so?"

Nate cursed and shook his head. "I can't take a chance you'll find out during a firefight and panic."

Eli was amused when Don took Nate's comment as an insult. Don's belligerence bristled all over him. "Sir..."

"Shut it and listen. The general tells me you have the clearance to hear and see what I'm going to share."

With a nod, Don stood at parade rest. Nate glanced at Eli. "Pull the shades, Eli. No point in sharing this more than we have to."

Eli walked to the window and whipped the curtains shut, his action putting him behind Don. When he turned back toward the center of the room, he frowned at Nate. "You or me?"

"I'll do it."

Eli nodded and took a step closer to Don. "Okay. Whenever you're ready."

*****

Don Dunn looked from one officer to the other, confused. They talked like something really big was about to happen, but for the life of him, he couldn't figure out what was going on. When Eli stepped closer, Don frowned at him. Muscles tense, Eli stood ready to...what?

"Look at me, soldier."

Don looked at Nate. "Sir?"

"Keep your eyes on me. Don't be afraid." Nate rolled his eyes. "Crap, I keep saying that to people, and it never works."

Eli laughed. "Never will. The shock is too much. Get it over with."

Don glanced at Eli and looked back at Nate. Nate nodded. When Nate shimmered, Don blinked. Nate shrank into a huge wolf; Don took an involuntary step backward, bumping into Eli's solid frame. "What the...?"

The wolf shimmered and once again, Nate stood in front of him. He didn't say anything, just watched Don. Don swallowed, then swallowed again. His heart thundered in his chest, but he had been afraid before. "Wow."

"Wow?"

"Yeah. Wow. How'd you do that?"

"I'm a werewolf. The people we are going after are werewolf hunters, killers. They've kidnapped another werewolf. If her father doesn't assassinate the president, they'll kill her." Nate shrugged. "I think they'll kill her, anyway."

"How would her father get to the president? Werewolves able to walk through fences and walls?"

"Only if they are the Secretary of Defense."

Don thought of Renate Bianchi. He had known her most of his life. Their families were friends, and her father recommended him for his first job. He thought of the times he escorted her to some political function or another. "You're trying to tell me Renate is a werewolf?"

"You know her?"

"We grew up on the same block. We're friends from way back." He felt his face settle into the look his family and friends called his stubborn face. "I don't believe it. You, yeah, I guess so, since I saw it, but not Renate."

He forced himself not to twitch beneath Nate's intense

gaze and jerked his chin toward Eli. "What about him? He a werewolf, too?"

"I am."

Dan looked around at the man standing behind him. The tall blonde man shimmered and shrank into a wolf. Though smaller than Nate's wolf, Eli's was larger than any wolf Don had seen in a zoo. He swallowed, keeping his gaze on Eli until he shifted back. "The general knows?"

"Yes."

"The general a werewolf, too?"

Nate and Eli shared an amused look, then both shook their heads. Nate answered his question. "No, the general isn't a werewolf."

"But he knows you are."

Nate nodded again. "He does, and he recruited us from retirement to take this assignment."

Don bowed his head, struggling to control his heartbeat. After a bit, he took a deep breath and looked up at Nate. "Renate is a friend, has been since third grade. Werewolf or not, if she's in trouble, I'm going with you."

Eli grinned and shrugged. "He has guts, Nate. And if you're too busy to open the cage, he could be handy. I can't handle silver like you can."

"Silver?" asked Don. Nate's intense gaze was back on him. Again, Don forced himself not to twitch.

"Renate is being held in a silver cage," said Nate. "Most werewolves can't handle silver. It burns them."

"But not you." Don raised an eyebrow and studied Nate. "So, what's different about you?"

Nate harrumphed. "Need to know, Corporal. Whatever happens, when we get there you just take care of business. You are not our target and are in no danger from either of us."

"Good to know, Sir. I'd hate to shoot superior officers."

Chapter 10

With no exterior window and no clock, Renate couldn't tell what time it was. The two men guarding her were relieved about an hour past. The two new men were more rested and less jumpy. Renate heard footsteps approach the bars to her cell and looked up. The guard facing her was younger than the others, with a friendlier attitude.

He held up a bottle. "Want some water?"

Renate glanced at the lid. It was still shut, the seal untampered. "Wouldn't mind it."

With a nod, he tossed the plastic bottle through the bars. She caught it. Her gaze stayed on him while she removed the lid and sniffed the water. Smelled clean.

The guard flushed. "I'll drink some of it if you're afraid of it."

Renate took a tiny sip. When she didn't taste anything that shouldn't be there, she took a long pull from the bottle. She could feel the cool liquid rush to replenish her dehydrated body. Replacing the cap on the bottle, she set it in the corner behind her. *Who knows how long it will be before I get more.* Her attention back on the guard, she tilted her head.

"You the one going to kill me?"

There was no disguising the shock in the young man's face. "What?"

"Don't talk to her, Marston." The other guard pulled both chairs back to the table. He frowned at the slab of meat sitting in the center of the card table and glanced at Renate. "Dog don't want no supper?"

The insult prickled, but Renate just grinned. "I like my

meat live."

The younger guard blinked, his face paling. He swallowed. "Live?

"I only eat the bad guys. You a bad guy, Marston?"

The minuscule shake of his head brought a grin to her face. "Then you should be okay."

Marston backed away, then nervously looked at his partner and licked his lips. "They didn't say anything about killing her."

"Not your hockey game. Not your puck." The other guard shrugged. "She's not human, Marston. It's like killing a dog."

Marston shook his head and muttered, "I like dogs."

The other guard turned to look at him. "You know I can't hear you when you mutter like that."

Marston ducked his head and looked at the floor. "I didn't say anything important." He turned his head to look at her.

Renate let her fear show briefly. She usually kept what she was feeling under control, enough so that others couldn't figure her out. She wanted this man to know she was scared. She tried to look helpless. It must have worked. He bit his lip and ducked his head again.

Marston's partner grumbled about the meat on the table and ordered him to clean it up. His face tight with disgust, he pulled a handkerchief from his pocket and used it to pick the meat up. After leaving for a few minutes to dispose of it, he returned with both hands clutching paper towels. The towels in one hand were wet, in the other hand dry. Quickly wiping the table clean, he gathered the damaged cards with the wet towels and dried the table.

Grunting, his partner drug a chair across the concrete

floor, the screech of it assaulting Renate's lupine ears. She frowned. Realizing she was getting stiff from sitting on the cold concrete, she stood up, stretched, and started pacing her small triangular cell.

"Sit back down."

She stopped and turned to face the older guard's frown. "Why?"

"If you don't want on the floor, sit on the bunk."

Renate pressed her lips together, then shook her head. "I won't use that flea trap." She glanced at Marston and sighed. He had moved to lean against the wall next to the door. His gaze moved from her to his partner. For a moment, she wondered if he would help her, then shook herself. Marston was one of them.

Somewhere outside the door, an alarm klaxon sounded. Marston's partner surged to his feet, knocking his chair over. He pulled his gun and turned toward her. As he brought the gun up, Renate heard a loud thunk. The guard's knees buckled, and he fell forward, his gun sliding across the floor toward the cell. Standing behind him, holding his gun by the barrel, Marston stood looking down at his partner, horror on his face.

Chapter 11

Careful to avoid touching the silver bars, Renate reached through and picked up the guard's gun, without taking her gaze from Marston. Marston's attention jerked up to her. Gun in hand, finger on the trigger, Renate waited to see what he would do.

Marston swallowed, then whispered, "He was going to shoot you."

Renate nodded. "And you?" Not that she was worried. Before he could reverse the gun in his hand and take a shot, she could pull the trigger.

Marston shook his head. "No one said anything about killing you. I...I won't do it."

"Can you open the cage?"

"They said you're dangerous."

"I am, but not to you." Shots rang out outside the small room. Renate motioned toward the door lock. "Open the door, Marston. It's your only chance."

More shots. Closer. Marston swallowed. Dropping his gun, he leaned over his partner and pulled a ring of keys off the man's belt. He rushed to the door and started trying the different keys. His hands were shaking so much Renate would have taken them from him and done it herself if not for the silver bars.

Shots came closer, then a loud growl filled the air. Marston almost dropped the keys, but finally found the right key. Just as he pulled the cage door open, the outer door burst open. A soldier with a bandana tied over his face rushed in, a wolf right behind him. The soldier brought the gun up just as Renate jumped through the door and stood between the soldier and Marston, her hands up. "Don't shoot!"

The wolf growled and took a step toward her. "You stay put," she ordered him. "He helped me. You will not hurt him."

The wolf stopped, sniffed, and looked from her to the man behind her. His mouth opened, showing his teeth. Taking another step toward her, he growled. *Mine!* burst into her mind. Startled, she took a step back, bumping into Marston. Marston's hands automatically caught her waist to keep her from falling when she slipped. *Mine!* The wolf jumped.

"Eli, Jabril, no!" At the command, the wolf twisted in the air, dropping a few feet in front of Marston. Renate looked up at another man standing at the door and shivered with the alpha strength behind the command. "Shift."

The order was directed at the wolf. He shimmered, becoming a blonde soldier. Knees bent, he stood as if he strained against the alpha's command, lethal intent in the gaze he fixed on the man behind Renate. She swallowed and stepped away from the man behind her, holding a hand up toward him. "Don't touch me, Marston. Back away. Slowly."

"What...?"

"You might live through this if you do as you're told." She didn't turn to look at him, but his gulp was audible. His steps shuffled back away from her until he bumped against the silver bars. Eyes still locked on the blonde man, Renate took a step forward.

"Renate?"

Blinking, she glanced at the bandana-hidden face of the soldier. He pulled the bandana off his face and grinned at her. "You okay?"

"Don." She didn't realize how much feeling she put into his name until the blonde growled again, this time at Don. She caught a glimpse of Don's frown before she jerked her gaze back to the blonde. "You are?"

"Name's Eli."

She opened her mouth and promptly closed it when the Alpha took another step into the room. "We don't have time for this, right now. Eli." The blonde looked at him. "Until or unless I give permission, you will not touch her." He waved toward Marston. "Or him. Understood?"

Renate shivered at the power behind the commands and wasn't surprised when Eli gave a reluctant nod. It would take someone more powerful than anyone Renate knew to defy that command. She swallowed, glanced at Eli, and frowned. *Mate?* In her mind, she felt her wolf, Salena, sit up and sniff toward Eli. Heard only by Renate, Salena howled her excitement. *Mate!*

This isn't the time or place, she told Salena. Salena ignored her, happily panting for Eli. Sighing, Renate looked at the alpha. "You are?"

"I'm Nate." He jerked his chin toward Marston. "He helped you?"

When she nodded, Nate sighed. "He'll have to come with us. They'll kill him if we leave him here."

Renate took a step toward the alpha. "He's the only one who tried to help me, I don't want him to die." Eli growled. Renate stopped and faced him. She frowned at him, then shoved the table aside and marched to him. She mashed her finger against his nose. "Listen you, I don't know you from the next guy. Marston helped me. That means *you* owe him. Got it?"

Eli blinked. She suddenly realized how ludicrous it must look for her, as petite as she was, to be ordering a hulking werewolf around. He nodded cautiously, eyes wide, then frowned at Nate's chuckles. Renate followed Eli's gaze with her own and studied Nate.

Nate shook his head. "I don't think you have a dog's show, Eli." He only laughed harder when Eli and Renate both growled at him.

Behind her, Marston cleared his throat. "Um, it won't take long for reinforcements to arrive. If you're going to leave, it should be soon."

Nate nodded. "Let's go, then."

"I..." Marston gulped. "I'm not sure I want to go with you."

Renate turned toward him. "If you stay, they'll kill you."

Marston shook his head. He took a step toward her. As he did, his partner's hand shot out and wrapped around his ankle, pulling him to the concrete floor. Marston cried out. His partner flipped him to his back and dove at him.

"Die, traitor!" Pulling a knife from his boot, his partner raised up to stab him. Marston caught the man's wrist in both his hands, struggling to keep the knife from his chest.

Howling her protest, Renate shimmered into a wolf. Snarling, she attacked the man wielding the knife, sinking her teeth deep into his forearm. Screaming, he dropped the knife, and it clattered to the floor. He rolled away from Marston, trying to shove Renate off him. She released his arm and jumped for his neck. His scream and the alpha's command to stop filled her ears.

Unable to disobey the alpha, Salena, Renate's wolf, whined and backed away from the man she attacked.

Moaning, he rolled to his knees, holding his arm. His eyes were wide, staring at the blood dripping down his sleeve. Gasping, his breath harsh, he looked up at Salena. "You made me one of you?"

Salena looked at the alpha as he walked past her.

Nate frowned. "It doesn't work that way, but your friends won't know that. Looks like you might want to get away, too, before they cage you." He shrugged. "Too bad you won't be able." He reached back and took Don's rifle from him. Swinging the rifle, he slammed the butt into the man's head. Before the guard hit the floor unconscious, Nate returned the rifle to Don and looked at Salena.

"Your father sent us to get you out."

Salena shifted into Renate and squinted at him. "How do I know you aren't just someone else trying to control my father?"

"Here." The word came from the hulking blonde.

Renate turned and looked at Eli. He pulled something wrapped in a bandana from his pocket. "Your dad sent this with us so you would know." He unwrapped the medallion. It was obvious he knew it was dangerous. He was careful not to touch the metal. Renate released her breath on a sigh. "Dad's medallion."

Eli nodded, rewrapped the medallion and returned it to his pocket. "We have to go."

"Marston goes with us."

Eli frowned at her, but when Nate agreed, he didn't comment. "He does. If he wants to live." Outside there were running feet. "Wolf up, guys." As Renate and Eli shimmered into wolves, he turned to Marston. "We don't have time for introductions or explanations. You have a better chance to survive with us, but I won't force you to come."

"Wow, Renate." Salena, Renate's wolf, glanced at Don. He looked a little pale, but he grinned at her wolf form. "You're beautiful, whatever your form."

When Jabril, Eli's wolf, growled again, Don looked from her to Jabril and raised an eyebrow before looking back at her. "Wish you'd told me. These guys are a bit much."

Salena barked her humor and gave Jabril a short growl. The big wolf stopped growling and whined. Nate laughed. "We'll have time to work everything out later."

"Um." Marston swallowed when the eyes of two wolves and two men focused on him. "There's a helicopter on the roof. I can't fly it, but if you guys can..."

Nate nodded. "To the roof, then. Lead the way."

Chapter 12

Jabril stayed close behind Salena. Her smell drove him almost insane with longing. Every time she looked at Don or Marston, he struggled to control his jealous growls. Confused, he kept an eye on the two humans. If Marston helped Renate, he did owe him for helping her. Eli, his human counterpart, didn't understand what he was feeling. Jabril was no help, he just kept repeating, *Mine,* every time he looked at her.

A door on their left shoved open and an armed man jumped through. Before Don could aim, Jabril knocked the man to the floor, teeth closed on his neck. *Mine! No one will harm mine!* When Jabril felt the man's neck snap, he dropped the lifeless man and ignored the fear rolling off Marston. Blood on his muzzle, Jabril barked at the man and hurried him after the others. If Nate wanted Marston alive, Eli would make sure Jabril kept him that way. For now, at least.

Nate led them into the stairwell. Don stopped and leaned over the rail, firing his rifle at men coming up the stairs below. Marston scrambled past Don. Jabril nudged Don's leg to keep him moving and followed when Don hurried after the others. Ahead, a dim light filtered through the door when Nate slammed it open. By the time Jabril followed them out onto the roof, the others were half-way to the helicopter.

Jabril sped up, racing for the pilot's seat. Shifting to man as he jumped into the helicopter, Eli started the machine without going through a safety check. Sometimes, you just have to pray everything is good. The rotors started turning. The chopper fuselage dipped first one way, then the other as his cohorts jumped into it, some on one side, some the other. He glanced back to see Renate shove Marston and Don further back, and he realized she was giving them the dubious extra protection of the fuselage walls. As humans, they wouldn't heal as well or as fast as werewolves.

Nate whirled his upright finger in the air to order take off. Eli nodded, turned back to the controls and started their ascent. Someone came running across the roof and jumped onto the landing gear on Eli's side. Pulling himself up, he reached inside the chopper. Instead of trying to climb inside, he grabbed hold of Renate. She didn't have her seatbelt fastened, yet, and he pulled her out of the helicopter, then dropped to land behind her. She shimmered into a wolf and jumped at him. A shot came from the doorway.

Eli cried out when the bullet hit Salena. She collapsed, shimmering back into her human form. Without considering his actions, Eli dove out of the helicopter toward them, shifting to wolf in mid-air. Behind him, Nate shouted his name, then started cursing. Jabril ignored him.

The man standing over Renate didn't have a gun and was unlikely to be much danger to her. Jabril rushed across the roof at the sniper who shot his mate. The man's fear stung Jabril's nose. As he charged the man, growls rending the air, the man turned his rifle on Jabril. Before he sighted in on Jabril, he fumbled the rifle. By the time he had control of it, it was too late. Jabril jumped, soaring through the air to knock him down. The gun clattered to the rooftop. He screamed once before Jabril caught him by the neck. Jabril shook him, his massive jaws and sharp teeth ripping the man's throat. When the man's neck snapped, Jabril dropped him and turned. Snout still dripping blood, eyes glowing red, he stalked toward the man hovering over his mate.

Eyes filled with terror, the man backed away from Renate. When Jabril reached her, he shimmered into his human form. His still glowing eyes on the man's face, Eli knelt and tried to pick her up. Nate's command not to touch her stopped him. Straining against the command, he twitched and frowned at his hand, unable to force it to reach her.

Footsteps brought his gaze up. The man jumped toward him. Don dropped out of the helicopter behind him. After a short struggle, the man threatening Renate and Eli collapsed to the rooftop. Don stood above him, the knife in his hand dripping blood.

Don wiped the knife on the dead man's sleeve, slipped the knife in the scabbard strapped to his thigh, and ran to them. "I'll get her."

Eli's eyes narrowed. He wiped the blood from his face on his left sleeve, a low growl resonating through his chest.

Don shook his head. "I won't hurt her. Just get in the chopper and fly it, man."

Steps echoed up the stairwell behind him. Eli nodded. "You hurt her, you die."

Don's jaw ticked, and he pursed his lips. He waited until Eli backed away, then gently picked up the unconscious girl, and carried her to the helicopter that once again settled to the rooftop. Marston reached out and helped Don pull her inside. Eli growled loud enough they heard him over the chopper blades. Both men glanced at him. As soon as she was buckled into her seat, they both raised their hands and backed away.

Eli rushed to the front door and climbed into the

pilot's seat. He glanced at the furious expression on his brother's face. Swallowing, Eli ignored him and worked the controls to lift away from the roof.

"You just jumped out and left us here." Nate's tight, angry tone shivered down Eli's spine.

"You know how to fly."

Nate's furious eyes glowed at him. "We'll discuss it later. Get us out of here."

Eli nodded. Guns roared. Most of the bullets missed the chopper, but two struck the fuselage, shattering the plexiglass. Increasing speed, Eli flew them toward the car they hid behind a wall of brush about a mile down the road. Once there, he set the chopper down in the center of the narrow road to block it. He jumped out and turned in time to see Nate transform his hand into Lycos' massive clawed hand. Nate swiped at the controls, claws tearing through metal, rubber, and plastic, rendering the controls useless.

"I can't touch her."

"What?" Nate, still angry, turned and looked at Eli.

"You told me not to touch her. I can't even pick her up."

Nate blinked, then his eyes grew wide with understanding. "You are released from the command, Eli, but you may not claim her until after we are safe, and only then if she approves."

Eli glared at Nate, but nodded, grateful he could at least carry her. Stepping to the back door, he leaned in and released her seatbelt. He slipped his arms beneath her knees and shoulders and carried her to the car. Nate ordered the other two to follow him. As far as Eli was concerned, someone else could drive the car. He was staying with Renate. He opened the back door, set Renate inside, then folded himself into the seat beside her. She moaned. He gently lifted her into his lap and put her head on his shoulder.

He glanced out the window when Nate pushed his door shut. Nate motioned for Don to drive and climbed into the front seat. Marston hesitated, then slid into the back seat next to Eli and Renate. When Eli looked at him, he raised his hands and leaned into his car door, as far away from Eli as he could get.

"Renate said you helped her."

Marston swallowed and nodded. "I stopped Roger when he tried to kill her, and I let her out of the cage."

Eli studied him. "For that, you have my thanks." He raised his chin and narrowed his eyes. "Don't touch her again."

"I won't. I promise."

Satisfied Marston wasn't a threat, Eli nodded, then looked down at the pale face of the woman his wolf called mate. No one told him this might happen. As mad as Nate was at him for diving out of the helicopter, Eli was even angrier. *Why didn't he tell me?*

Jabril was no help. He kept whining, eager to claim his mate. Without Nate's restriction, Eli wasn't sure he could keep his wolf from taking the girl in his lap as his. Eli fingered her dark hair, stroked her pale face, and sighed. *Looks like things will be interesting for a while.*

Chapter 13

It was dark by the time they got back to Calgary. At Nate's direction, Don pulled into a shady looking motel. Nate went inside and rented two rooms for the night, asking for rooms away from the street. When he returned to the car, he directed Don to pull around to the back. One dim streetlamp illuminated the back parking lot. Don pulled into a spot close to their rooms.

Nate glanced at Don. "Stay here a minute."

Don nodded. Nate stepped out. A moment later, a blue light flashed across the parking lot and exploded the bulb in the streetlight. Marston gasped behind him and Don frowned. *What was that?*

Nate leaned back into the car. "Let's go."

Without the streetlamp shining on them, they moved in almost total darkness to the room Nate indicated. He motioned for Eli to carry Renate inside, then waved Don and Marston to follow. Nate closed the door after he entered behind them. Lights still off, Nate moved to the window and studied the terrain outside for several minutes, before Don saw his shadow nod. The curtains were drawn tight, and Nate flipped the switch by the door, lighting the room.

"Put her down."

Thankful the anger in Nate's tone wasn't directed at him, Don watched as Eli frowned and gently lowered Renate to the bed. When Eli stood back up, Nate marched across the room and punched him in the gut. Eli bent over, holding his stomach, coughed twice, then looked up at Nate without standing up. "Feel better?"

"You know I don't want to fly!"

"But I knew you could." Eli straightened, his chin jutting out. "They had my mate, Nate. I couldn't let them take her."

Unconsciously, Don backed away from the two, then almost laughed when he realized Marston matched him step-for-step. Nate huffed and glared at Eli. Don frowned. If someone hit him like that, they would be in a fight. If he wasn't down for the count.

Instead of swinging at Nate, Eli glared right back at him. "What would you have done if it was Janelle they had?"

Nate blinked, then blinked again. The anger left his expression almost immediately. Taking a deep breath, he looked past Eli at the girl. "Are you sure?"

"No. Yes." Eli shrugged. "Jabril is sure." For a moment, he looked lost. "Why didn't you tell me?"

Don glanced at Marston. He seemed as fascinated by the drama as Don felt. Turning his gaze back to the others, Don frowned. "Uh, guys, what's going on?"

Nate threw a quick glance at Don and Marston, then sighed. Ignoring them, he turned back to Eli. "I didn't know it would hit you like that. I don't know much more about this stuff than you do."

Eli took a deep breath, let it out slowly. He nodded. "I have to treat her wound."

"I'm a trained medic." Don flinched from the look Eli speared him with.

"I'll treat the wound."

Don swallowed and nodded. "Whatever you say, Eli. Just let me know if you need help."

Eli gave him a sharp nod, then turned and lifted Renate to slip her vest off her shoulders. He caught his breath, and

Don moved to see that removing the vest caused her shoulder to bleed again. "Sure you don't need help? It looks like the bullet is still in there."

Eli moved to touch her shoulder. His hand started shaking and twitching. Eye's wide, he looked up at Nate. "I think the bullet is silver."

Nate cursed, then nodded. "I'll protect you. Get it out."

Protect him? Don looked at Marston. Marston raised his shoulders in a shrug to let him know he was just as confused as Don was. Looking back, Don gasped. Nate was glowing with a light blue light, the same blue as the light that blew up the bulb in the streetlamp. Nate touched Eli's shoulder, and after a moment, Eli, too, was glowing.

Eli swallowed and nodded. He pulled a Case knife from his pocket and unfolded the blade. Swallowing again, he carefully inserted the tip of the blade into the wound. Renate moaned and opened her eyes. She stared at Eli for a second, then nodded and closed her eyes again. Jaw clenched, she didn't move while he dug out the bullet. When it popped out of the wound, Nate reached around Eli and picked it up. The glow faded first from Eli, then from Nate.

Renate opened her eyes, looked at Eli, and whispered. "Thank you."

Eli started to touch her face but stopped. He held up his hands, showing her the blood. "I'll get some towels to clean you up."

When Eli went to the small bathroom to wash his hands and get some wet and dry towels to clean her wound, Don stepped toward her. He didn't dare come very close, but he needed to make sure his childhood friend was okay.

"Renate?"

Renate turned her face toward him. A soft smile lit her face. "Hello, Don. Dad send you, too?"

"Yeah, him and the general. They didn't tell me it was you we were after, though."

Renate grinned. "Sounds like them." She held her right arm tight against her and pushed herself up higher on the bed until she could lean against the head of the bed frame.

"We need to get you to a hospital." Don could hear the worry in his tone and was confused when she laughed.

"No. No hospital. Now that the bullet is out, I'll heal fast enough." She turned her attention back to Eli as he sat on the bed beside her. Leaning her head away from him, she let him gently wash the wound with the wet cloth. With the blood gone, Eli carefully wiped her shoulder with the dry towel.

"What happened to your wound?" Don hated the squeak in his voice, but couldn't help it. "The wound is almost gone!"

"I'm a werewolf, Don." She shrugged. As carefully as she moved, Don thought the shoulder must still be tender. "Unless there is silver in a wound, it heals pretty fast. By tomorrow morning, it'll be almost completely well."

"Handy."

She laughed at him. "It helps when you've been shot."

"So I see."

Nate cleared his throat and waved his cell phone, catching everyone's attention. "I'm going to call the general and let him know we have Renate. Renate, your dad will probably want to talk to you."

After reporting in, Nate handed the phone to Renate. "Hi, Dad. Yes, I'm okay. I'll tell you all about it when we get back." She glanced at Eli and frowned at his intense stare. "I'm safe. These guys will make sure I get back home." She hesitated. "You didn't do what they wanted you to, did you?"

Eli, Nate, and Don all held their breaths, waiting for his reply. Marston, when she looked at him, just looked confused. "Good." With a loud sigh, she gave the guys a thumbs up. "You did the right thing, sending these guys after me. Yes, they are behaving themselves." She bit her lip and looked straight at Eli. His face colored. She turned her back to Eli and Nate. Don almost grinned when he realized she was hiding her smile from Eli. "Okay. See you tomorrow. Good night." She ended the call and turned to hand the phone back to Nate. "He wants you to bring me back to the compound."

Nate nodded. "The plane is waiting for us in Seattle. We'll leave in the morning. You need to heal, first." He ran his fingers through his hair and scratched his head. "Don, you stay in here with Renate and Eli."

When Don cast a doubtful glance at Eli, Nate followed that with an order to the werewolf. "Eli, remember what I told you. And don't attack Don. He won't hurt her."

Eli looked at Don. Don swallowed, then Eli nodded. "I won't hurt him."

"Good. The general wants him back alive." Nate turned to Marston. "You're next door with me." Marston glanced at Don. Don shrugged. Nate ignored the exchange of looks. "We leave at first light."

"How do we get back across the border with two extras?" Don motioned toward Marston and Renate.

Nate grinned. "Renate will be able to run tomorrow. We'll let her and Eli run through the wilderness and meet us on the other side of the border. Marston will take Eli's place in the car. Marston can use Eli's id"

Marston sputtered. "They'll know I'm not Eli."

Sitting on the bed, Eli laughed. "Not if Nate tells them you're me."

Don raised an eyebrow. "What?"

Nate nodded. "They'll believe Marston is Eli." After glancing at Marston, Nate frowned. "Have any extra clothes he can wear, Don? Maybe some jeans and a t-shirt? I don't think Eli's or mine would fit him."

Don turned to study Marston. Marston's build was more like his own. Both were fit and well-muscled. He compared his own build to Eli and Nate. As proud as he was of the muscles he built over the years, the two werewolves were even more muscular. Don figured they could probably win an Ironman competition, no sweat. "I think so. And you're right. Your clothes would hang off him."

"Have two?" Eli shrugged. "Renate needs a shirt, too."

Don glanced at Eli and nodded. "I'll get one for her, too. Yours would swallow her."

Chapter 14

Nadrai woke Janelle. *Someone is in the house.* Frowning, Janelle glanced at the alarm clock on the bedside table. *At 2 in the morning?* Before Nadrai could answer, Janelle stilled as slow footsteps softly padded down the hall toward her bedroom door. *Call Dusty, Jonathan, and Ben.*

Janelle slipped quietly out of bed, arranged the pillows beneath the blankets to make it appear she still slept and crept to the closet. She didn't have to worry about humans, but the smell outside her door identified him as a werewolf. Another sniff and she knew it was Bradley. Janelle reached inside the closet for the pistol Nate insisted she keep loaded and nearby. Without silver bullets, it would only be fatal to him if it was a headshot, but it should stop him long enough for the men to arrive. Quietly, she checked the magazine, then slipped off the safety. As her door swung open without making a sound, she turned to face Bradley.

He didn't see her. He shut the door with a faint click of the latch bolt. The smell of her still hung over the bed. She watched him creep toward the bed. The silver-bladed knife in his hand caught the moonlight shining through the open window, reflecting a glimmer over his face. Eyes narrowed in determination, he jumped forward and stabbed at her pillow.

Janelle flipped on the light. Bradley spun, the knife still in his hand. The pistol in her right hand aimed at his chest, she nodded at the knife. "Drop it."

He sneered at her. "You can't kill me with that unless you can make a headshot."

Left hand pressed against her stomach, protecting her

unborn child, she raised one eyebrow. "You think I can't? Take another step and you'll find out."

Roaring, he jumped at her. Janelle aimed at his chest. A headshot would kill him, but a chest shot should incapacitate him. At least briefly. She could smell his breath before she pulled the trigger. Fire shot out the muzzle and the bullet slammed into his shoulder. He staggered back, caught himself, and moved toward her again. Frowning, wishing there was another way, Janelle moved the angle of her pistol and shot him in the left eye.

As the bullet slammed him to the floor, her door crashed open. Jonathan, dressed in tighty whities, was shoved from behind as Dusty and Ben pushed into the room. Shirtless, Dusty and Ben sported pajama pants. Tig charged in behind them, barking. The three men were ready for anything when they barged in. After taking a look at Janelle, right arm dropped to her side, pistol dangling from her fingers, left hand still cradling her unborn child, they lost their protective stances. Dusty shushed Tig.

She looked up as Jonathan reached down and plucked the pistol from her fingers. Tears pooled in her eyes. "I never shot anyone before, Jonathan."

He nodded, clicked the safety on, and tossed the gun to her bed. Bending, he lifted her in his arms, carried her out of the room and downstairs. Dusty and Ben followed close behind. The wolf kids had all gathered downstairs. As Jonathan settled her onto the couch, the front door burst open. Flora ran in, followed by Will and the other adult werepanthers.

"Janelle, are you alright?" The fear in Flora's voice was strident. Jonathan backed away and let Flora get to Janelle.

When Flora wrapped her arms around her Alpha

Queen, Janelle caught her breath and buried her face in Flora's shoulder. She couldn't stop shaking. "I killed him."

"Who? Who did you kill?"

"Bradley. He tried to stab me, and I killed him."

Flora pulled back. She caught Janelle's face in her hands. "Look at me, Janelle." Janelle shook her head and tried to pull away. Flora's hold grew tight enough it was painful. "Look at me!"

Janelle sniffed and focused on Flora.

"You didn't have a choice."

Nodding, Janelle swallowed. "I know, but..." She felt tears tracking her face. It wouldn't do for the kids to see her crying.

Flora sighed. Vaguely, she heard Flora call for Dottie. A minute later, Dottie sat on the other side of her. The two women held her steady between them. "We're right here, Janelle."

Nadrai ordered everyone but Jonathan, Dusty, Ben, and Will to go back to their beds. After everyone else cleared the room, Jonathan, Dusty, Will, and Ben stood guard outside each entrance to the living room. Janelle's sobs started. For long minutes, she cried, wishing Nate was with her. When she could finally control herself, she sniffed and leaned back. Looking from Flora to Dottie, she smiled through the tears still on her face. "I'm sorry."

Dottie stroked her hair. "Don't be. Killing someone shouldn't be easy. If it was, there would be something wrong with you."

"But I'm a wolf, and..."

"Yes," interrupted Flora. "You're a wolf. A pregnant wolf. You would be upset even if you weren't pregnant, but right now, you have all these extra hormones. And I'm sure you were as frightened for your pup as for yourself." Flora gave her a sad smile. "At least it wasn't someone you used to care about."

Janelle caught her breath at the pain in Flora's eyes. To protect Ben, her father, the wolfpack, and the werepanther clowder, Flora had challenged her aunt, the woman who raised her, for the queen's title. Her aunt died in that battle. "I'm sorry," Janelle whispered to Flora. "I didn't understand."

Flora smiled gently. "It's part of life in the clowder. And in the pack, too, for that matter. If you were gone, Nate would be distraught. I'm sure Bradley thought that would give him a chance when he challenged Nate." She glanced at Dottie. "Do we have some chamomile tea?"

Dottie nodded and stood up. "I'll go fix us all a cup." Her smile was shaky, too. "I think we could all use it."

Janelle caught her breath. "What about his family?"

Flora patted her shoulder. "We'll worry about them when they get here."

"Do you know when they'll arrive?"

"Tomorrow afternoon."

Janelle felt tears flood her eyes again. "How will I tell them I killed him?"

Chapter 15

When Eli slipped into the bed beside her, Renate didn't argue. He saw Don's frown, but thankfully he didn't say anything. Eli knew the other man wasn't happy. And he was pretty sure her dad would be furious. Eli motioned at the other bed. "You sleep over there, Don. Get the lights, will you?"

Still frowning, Don walked to the door, flipped off the lights, and went to the other bed. Don removed his boots, dropped them one at a time to thud on the floor, then stretched out on the bed.

It didn't surprise Eli when Don rolled to his side facing the other bed. He knew that if Renate decided she didn't want him beside her, Don would try to move him. Eli grinned. Brave man.

Turning his back to Don, Eli gently touched Renate's face. Wearing Don's shirt, she smelled like Don. Jabril growled. Eli sighed. He didn't like Don's scent on her, either, but there was nothing else for her to wear. Jabril would just have to get over it. "Do you need anything?"

"No."

Her low voice filled him with longing. Thankful for his wolf vision, he studied her face. He cleared his throat. "Will you let me know if you do?"

She looked at his eyes. *Mine!* Eli swallowed and grinned at her. "I'm sorry. I don't quite understand what's happening."

"You are not wolf-born?"

"No. This is pretty new to me."

"Who changed you?"

"Nate did, but it wasn't on purpose." When she gave him a disbelieving look, he grinned. "Nate's my foster-brother. We decided to be blood-brothers when we were just kids." He shrugged. "Didn't either one of us know he was a wolf, at that point."

She frowned. "How's that possible?"

"Nate's folks died when he was young. To protect him from Jackson, his step-dad abandoned him to the human foster care system. My family fostered him. Nate has a medallion like your dad's. It repressed his change until after he met his mate, Janelle, so, no, he didn't know until March. I found out about two weeks after he did."

"I never met a changeling before. You only just found out in the past month or so?"

"Yeah." Eli shifted a little to ease the cramp in his shoulder. "We've both had a lot to learn really fast. This thing between us..." He cleared his throat. "I don't really understand it, and Jabril just keeps repeating the word 'Mine.' Do you...do you feel it, too?"

Renate laughed. "Yes, I feel it. Salena is doing the same thing."

"She is?"

"Yes." She closed her eyes. "If I'm going to be healed enough to run cross-country tomorrow, I need some sleep."

Eli smiled. "Get some rest. I'll keep you safe."

Eyes still closed, she nodded. "I had a feeling you would."

*****

Just before daylight, Nate knocked on the door. Renate wasn't sure how she knew it was him. She just did. She sleepily opened one eye and watched Eli roll off the bed and walk to the door. Nate walked in, with Marston behind him. As the door closed, Renate sat up and glanced at the other bed. Don was sitting up, pulling on his boots. "Good morning," she said around a yawn.

Don nodded and glanced at Eli before answering her. "Good morning. Sleep good?"

"I did." She looked up at Eli and smiled. "Better than I have in ages." Don's t-shirt billowed around her. With a frown, she tied a knot in the fabric over her left hip, making it fit better.

Eli grinned. "Good. Feel up to that run?"

Renate rolled her shoulder, trying to loosen up the stiffness that set in overnight. "I think so. Shifting will help speed up the healing." She grinned back at him. "What's for breakfast? It seems like days since I ate anything."

When Eli caught his breath in concern, she rolled her eyes. "I wasn't hungry last night, so don't go all worried about me. I am hungry this morning. So, what's for breakfast?"

Eli looked at Nate. Nate shrugged. "The restaurant across the street has waffles and eggs. Will that do?"

When Eli looked back at her, his eagerness to please her annoyed her. "Would you quit that?"

"What?"

She laughed at his baffled expression and nodded. "Waffles and eggs sound great."

Two hours later, the five of them were headed south toward Grasmere to the Roosville Border Crossing. Now that she was almost well, she sat beside Eli, instead of in his lap. Anytime Don drove around a corner, Eli glared at Marston for getting too close to her. By the time they stopped again for gas, Marston was trembling constantly. When Marston excused himself to go to the restroom, she turned to Eli.

"You have got to stop that."

"Stop what?"

"You're scaring poor Marston to death."

"He gets too close to you."

Renate blew out a loud breath. "If he gets any further away from me, he'll be riding outside the car! He can't help it that the road is so curvy."

Eli's chagrined expression made her sigh and speak more softly. "Look. He knows you don't like it. He's not trying to touch me. If you don't like it so much, you ride in the middle."

"I'm too big to ride in the middle." He ducked his head and peeked at her. "You could ride in my lap."

In the front seat, Nate snickered. Don stopped breathing for a moment. Renate glared at the back of their heads, then looked at Eli. "Fine. If it means you'll give the poor guy a break, I'll sit in your lap."

She laughed when Eli blinked at her. Without giving her a chance to recant, he picked her up and settled her in his lap. If he'd been a cat, he'd have been purring. She shook her head and leaned against him. His arms circled her.

With a contentment she couldn't remember ever feeling before, she put her head on his shoulder. When Marston opened the door and slid onto the seat, Eli didn't so much as look at him. After a moment, she heard Marston's soft breath releasing his tension.

She grinned. Her mate was so possessive and territorial. That thought trickled into her mind, and she jerked to an upright position. Eli leaned back and looked down at her. Looking up at him, she swallowed. *Eli really is my mate.* Joy curled around her, like the mist of a low fog, and seeped deep into her. *Mine!* Salena yelped her happiness. Eli's slow smile sent shivers down her back.

There was no going back, now.

Chapter 16

Janelle looked up from her laptop when Flora tapped on the office door and stuck her head in. "Will called on his walkie talkie to let us know Bradley's family just pulled in the front gate."

Suddenly uninterested in her homework, Janelle saved her work and shut the laptop. She took a deep breath and looked at Flora. "I don't know what to tell them."

Flora sucked her bottom lip into her mouth and nodded. "Want one of us to tell them?"

Janelle thought of Bradley's attack. Memories of his blood and brains splattered on her walls and bedroom furniture swamped her mind. Swallowing, she forced her thoughts away from the blood. She hated blood. Always had. As much as she had seen over the past months, she was sure she always would. She was thankful Dusty and Jonathan offered to clean her room. Even so, she wouldn't be staying in there until Nate returned.

She shivered and shook her head. "I'll talk to them."

Flora nodded and followed her down the stairs, and out the front door. When Janelle hesitated at the steps, Flora touched her arm. "I'm right here with you."

Janelle sent her friend a grateful smile and stepped down off the porch as Mrs. Bradley opened the moving van door and jumped to the ground. Her eyes darted around the compound, searching, Janelle was sure, for her husband. Taking a deep breath, Janelle squared her shoulders and walked up to the woman just as a teenage boy and two blonde little girls came around the front of the truck to join their mother.

"Mrs. Bradley? You are welcome to the ranch."

Mrs. Bradley's gaze scanned around the compound again and frowned. "Where is Trent?"

"Your husband?"

"Yes. Where is Trent?"

Janelle bit her lip, then frowned. "I'm sorry to tell you this, Mrs. Bradley. Your husband died last night."

"Died?" Mrs. Bradley blinked and looked around as if she thought she was in a trap. "Trent died?"

Dusty stepped up beside Janelle, Tig beside him. "If I may?"

Janelle swallowed and nodded. Dusty took another step to make it easier to protect Janelle should the widow attack. "Your husband attacked our Alpha Queen last night. She killed him in self-defense."

"Trent's dead?"

Janelle tilted her head, studying the woman. Either she didn't understand what she was told, or his death didn't make her unhappy. The woman took a step toward Janelle. "You killed him?"

"He attacked me with a silver knife."

"And you killed him."

Janelle nodded.

"You're sure he's dead?"

"I'm sure."

Mrs. Bradley took a shaky breath, then sank to her knees. She bowed her head and started crying. For a moment, Janelle felt so sorry for her, then the woman looked up. "Thank you," she whispered. "I couldn't do it, but someone needed to."

Janelle felt a reflection of her own shock roll off Dusty and Flora. "What?"

"I told Jackson and Jackson just laughed. Said as pack alpha, it was Trent's right to do what he wanted to." She put her face in hands for a moment, then turned and pulled her girls into her arms. "It's okay, my sweethearts. Daddy can't hurt you, anymore."

Confused, Janelle looked at the boy, remembering Bradley told Nate his son was fifteen. He looked relieved, too, though he didn't join his mom and sisters in crying. He gave a shuddering breath and looked at Janelle. "Dad's been abusing my sisters for years, and no one, not Mom, not me, could make him stop. The only one who might have been able to...refused." He touched his mother's head tenderly and looked up at Janelle. "We have no home. Dad was so awful to the pack, we aren't welcome there, anymore."

Janelle nodded and asked Nadrai to call Adrian and Reese to the house. "You are welcome here. What's your name?"

"Trent." His voice was bitter. "But I hate having my dad's name, so my friends call me Trey."

"Trey, we have a house almost ready for your family. You will stay here, as part of this pack."

For the first time, Trey's eyes watered. "Thank you."

The two teens she called ran up. Reese raised an eyebrow. "You wanted us, Janelle?"

"Yes, Reese. This is Trey. Trey's family will be living with us." She caught Reese's gaze with her own. "Understand. This is Trey's family. They are now part of this pack."

Reese nodded and grinned at Trey. "Welcome."

Janelle looked at Trey. His eyes were wide. He cleared his throat, and tried to speak, but didn't seem to be able to. Janelle put her hand on his shoulder. "Your father's memory is banished. We will only speak of him one time more when the Alpha returns. Pending approval by the Alpha, your family is now pack. Welcome, Trey."

Trey's mother released her daughters and stood up. Blinking back her tears, she gave Janelle a trembling smile. "I thank you. My family thanks you."

Janelle gave her a gentle smile. "I'll ask the bears to get your house ready, first, so you won't have to spend much time in tents. Nate told them to put it over near the pond." Janelle pointed. "Does that sound good to you?"

"Yes. Anywhere is fine." She glanced at Trey then looked back at Janelle. "Did you say bears?"

"She did." The former Execution Squad leader stepped forward, his gaze intent on Mrs. Bradley. "Hello, Nettie."

"Hello." Mrs. Bradley's face colored and she bowed her head. Head still down, she turned back to Janelle. "You must think me awful, not to be able to protect my own children."

Janelle curled her fingers under the other woman's chin and raised her face. "I think you are very brave to have tried to protect them. You are welcome here. The entire pack will protect you all." She released her chin.

Flora took a step to put her even with Janelle. "Your name is Nettie?"

Mrs. Bradley smiled. "Annetta, but yes, most people call me Nettie."

Flora glanced at Janelle. Janelle nodded. "I'm Flora. We were told you're a school teacher. We need another teacher in the school here. Are you interested?"

"Really?" Nettie's face lit up. "I love teaching, especially the young kids."

"That's perfect. We need a pre-school and early

elementary teacher. After you get settled into your new home, we'll have a meeting and get everything set up."

Nettie looked at Trey and grabbed his arm. He laughed at the excitement on his mom's face. "See, Mom. I told you when the council dissolved that things would be better."

Chapter 17

Jabril ran through a snow-covered forest glade and howled into the wind. Salena ran beside him. Her howls joined his. Together, they ran through the pine trees, stopping occasionally to frolic in the snow. A scent he didn't know caught Jabril's attention. Nose to the ground, he followed the trail, until he rounded a boulder and came upon a black bear cub. The cub stumbled away from him and bleated for his mother.

Startled, Jabril stood still and stared. Ears forward, he tilted his head. The mother bear roared and reared up on her hind legs. Just before she charged him, Salena barked and bumped him. Together, they ran from the bear, barking in glee with the excitement, cold wind ruffling their fur.

Soon, they outran the bear and she turned back to her cub. Salena barked and jumped on Jabril, rolling with him in the snow. Jabril rolled with her until he stood over her. Suddenly, the fun was over. Trembling with the need to disobey Nate, Jabril licked his mate's neck. She stilled beneath him, seemed to be waiting.

Whining, he backed off. Salena scrambled to her feet and studied her mate, tongue hanging out. Yipping a laugh at him, she spun and raced toward the pickup point. Jabril growled playfully and sped after her, exhilarated by the chase.

*****

Six miles south of the Roosville Border Crossing, Don pulled the car to the side of the road and turned off the engine. As before, Nate rode shotgun, and Marston rode in the back. Don looked at Nate. "How long will it take them to get here?"

Nate shrugged. "Shouldn't be too long. Wolves travel about 35 miles per hour, and werewolves are at least twice that fast. Wouldn't be surprised if they beat us here since it took a while to go through checkpoints at Roosville."

"Yeah. Just how did you do that, anyway?"

Nate glanced at him. "You wouldn't believe me if I told you."

"Try me."

"It was magic."

"You expect me to believe that?"

A smile tugged at Nate's lips. "I knew you wouldn't believe me." He looked around and waved at the trees. "And there they are."

Two wolves bounded toward the car, both larger than normal wolves. When they arrived, they looked both ways to check for observers, then quickly shifted into their human forms. Eli opened the back door, slid inside, and then helped Renate climb into his lap. He pulled the door shut. "We're ready whenever you are."

Don shook his head and started the car. After two stops for gas and another for a meal, twelve hours later Don turned into the Seattle airport. They climbed the steps into the plane and latched their seatbelts. Soon they were in the air. Don glanced at the other four, then leaned back in his chair and closed his eyes. He was tired, and they still had a six-hour trip ahead.

*****

When they arrived at the underground compound, they were escorted back to the same room Nate and Eli were in when they met with the general and the secretary. The table was replaced with a larger table and enough chairs for the five to sit while they waited. After an hour, the door opened and the general entered, followed by Secretary Bianchi.

"Daddy!" Renate jumped up from her chair to give her dad a hug. The secretary caught her and held her tight, his eyes shut, relief filling him. When she squirmed to get loose, he let her go.

"Are you alright, Renate?"

Renate grabbed his hand with both hers and smiled. "I'm fine, Dad."

He looked over her head and nodded at Nate, Eli, and Don. "Thank you." When his gaze settled on Marston, he frowned. He nodded toward him. "Who's he?"

Renate glanced around to see who he was pointing out. "His name is Marston. He helped me get away. Without him, I'd have been shot."

Sitting beside Marston, Eli shook his head and muttered, "Happened anyway."

Bianchi gaze snapped to Eli. "What did you say?"

"Uh, Dad, I was kind of, uh, shot, on the way out."

"What?" He caught her shoulders and held her away from him, visually searching to ensure she was okay.

"I'm okay, Dad. Eli and Don saved me. Eli removed the bullet from my shoulder, and I'm fine, now. Really."

"Eli did? But Don's a medic." He looked at Don. "Why didn't you take care of her?"

Don caught his lip between his teeth and glanced at Eli. Bianchi followed his gaze and frowned. "What's going on here?"

"Dad."

Bianchi looked down at his daughter. When she swallowed, he frowned. "What is it, Renate?"

"I, uh, well, you see, I..."

"Renate's my mate."

At Eli's words, Renate gave her dad a hopeful grin and shrugged. "That's what I was trying to say."

The secretary looked at Eli, expressionless, then looked at his daughter. "You were claimed?"

She shook her head. "Not yet, but..." She swallowed. "Salena and I both accept him, Dad. He's my mate."

Bianchi pressed his lips together and she shivered beneath his piercing gaze. He shook his head. "Unacceptable. Your engagement has been arranged to another."

"What? Who?"

Renate's father ignored Eli's sharp intake of breath. "Jackson's son is Alpha to the Arkansas pack now that Jackson is dead. As our new Alpha, he commands you to be his mate. Nothing can be done."

Behind Renate, Eli's chair hit the floor. "No! She's mine."

Bianchi looked past Renate, fixing his gaze on Eli. "She has no choice. The decision is made."

Chapter 18

Nate stood and caught Eli's shoulder in his right hand, forcing him to stay put. Koreth gave Jabril command to wait. Muscles tight, ready to fight if necessary, Eli stood still. When Nate was sure Eli wouldn't attack the secretary, he released him and turned to face the secretary and the general. "Renate is old enough to decide for herself which mate she wants, Secretary."

The secretary raised one corner of his lip. "Just because you did your duty and returned her to me, don't think you have the right to an opinion in this." The secretary turned to General Brighton. "I want these men detained until we leave." He pointed to Marston. "And arrest him as an enemy spy."

Brighton nodded and turned toward the door.

Nate raised an eyebrow. "I don't think you want to do that, Secretary."

Brighton whipped around. "Watch it, Rollins. You're on pretty shaky ground, yourself."

"Shaky ground, General? This man helped us. If not for him, Renate would have died before we got to her. He also helped the rest of us escape. He's under my personal protection. You can't have him."

A vein on the general's temple throbbed with his anger. Ignoring him, Nate looked at the secretary. "As for your daughter, she, too, is under my protection. If she doesn't want to mate with Jackson's son, I won't allow it." Beside him, Nate felt the tension in Eli relax.

The general took a step toward Nate. "You are under arrest for treason, Rollins." His voice took on a graveled sound as he said, "My sources say after you killed Jackson, you disappeared. You didn't mention that before."

Nate rubbed the back of his neck and sucked on his teeth. "From my point of view, everyone else disappeared."

Eli snickered, then cleared his throat and rearranged his face into an emotionless mask when Nate frowned at him.

"Where did you go?"

"I don't know, General. They didn't tell me."

"Who are they?"

Nate ignored the general and looked at the Secretary. *That is not for humans to hear.* When Koreth sent the thought to the secretary's wolf, the secretary blinked, then his eyes opened wide.

"How did you...," he started to whisper, then turned to the general. "Those two," he pointed at Don and Marston, "send them to the room next door. Now."

The general frowned. "Secretary..."

"I want them out, General. Now!"

Face still tight with anger, the general nodded and scratched his ear. He looked at Don. "Take Marston to the room next door and stay there until I come get you."

"Sir, yes, Sir." Don stood and caught Marston by the shoulder. "Let's go."

"But..."

"Let's go." Don pulled him to his feet and yanked him to the door. A moment later, the door shut behind them.

The cameras and mics are no longer working, Nate. Nate nodded. *Thanks, Koreth.* Leaning forward, Nate ignored the general, keeping his gaze locked on the secretary's eyes. "The one who spoke said she was the First Mother, Mother to the Lycos." He stopped for a second and raised his right eyebrow. "You sure you want to know the rest?"

"The First..." Bianchi swallowed. "You're sure she was the First Mother?"

"You want to know?"

Bianchi gave him a nervous nod.

"You are in no danger."

Both his superiors looked startled. Renate frowned. The general took a step toward Nate. "What are you talking about?" He stopped when Bianchi caught him by the shoulder with a tight-knuckled grip.

Nate stood up, leaned his head back, and called his Lycos form, just barely remembering to phase his camos to keep from ripping them when his tail thrust out behind him. Bianchi craned his neck back to look up at Nate's wolf-man form towering over him, his mouth gaping open. Renate cried out and covered her mouth with both hands.

Brighton cursed and turned toward the door, but Bianchi jerked him to a stop. The general looked at Bianchi, then looked again at Nate. Hand still gripping Brighton's shoulder, Bianchi started to fall to his knees.

"Don't do that, Secretary."

As if he was a puppet and the puppeteer jerked his strings taut, the secretary stood straight. "You...You're...How?"

Nate, as Lycos, shrugged, then shimmered into his human form. "I'm a Royal."

Bianchi's eyes were huge. "The missing Royal child? That's you?"

Nate scratched the whiskers on his face and sighed. "Never been called that. My father was Jackson's twin brother, Grant. Does that answer your question?"

His eyes even larger in his face, the secretary nodded.

"The First Mother gave you charge?"

"She did." Nate rubbed the back of his neck. "My charge is to protect *were* from human and human from *were*."

"What the...?" The general broke off when the secretary shook him.

"Stay quiet, man. Don't you know who he is?" At the question in the general's expression, Bianchi sighed. "He's Lycos, the Royal, the Were King." Expression rueful, he shrugged. "In all things *were* and paranormal, Brighton, Rollins outranks us both." He looked at Nate and bit his lip. "I've already accepted Renate's engagement."

"Protecting *were* includes protecting Renate. Even from you, Secretary."

"But I...she..."

When Bianchi trailed off, Nate shook his head. "I have disbanded the Were Council. Until I have time to meet with all the heads of *were* and others, I run things. I won't put compulsion of obedience on you, Secretary, but if you disobey, you'll answer to me."

Nate glanced at Eli and then at Renate. "Renate, I don't know Jackson's son, but if he's like his father, he is not worthy of you. You may choose your mate."

Renate glanced at her father, then walked to stand by Eli. Eli's arm slipped around her waist and she leaned against him. "I'm sorry, Dad, but I choose Eli."

Bianchi swallowed. "You understand the consequences, Renate? To go against the Alpha..."

Nate leaned toward Bianchi. "Renate and Eli will mate at the ranch, tomorrow morning." A surge of emotion from Renate and Eli washed over him. "We might as well take care of any possible problems, though. Just before we head to the ranch, send a message to Jackson's pup and let him know he's invited to the mating. He's welcome to try to stop it. I'll take care of it from there." Nate studied the two men in front of him. "You're both invited, too." His lips curved in a mirthless grin. "In fact, I insist you attend."

Chapter 19

Nate decided only the four he brought back from Canada, the general, and the secretary would go to the ranch. Since the general and secretary wouldn't have a pilot to fly them back, the military chopper carrying them landed in San Antonio. Nate rented a large SUV and loaded everyone inside.

Eli and Renate took the back two bucket seats. Marston sat in front of Eli. Renate's dad and the general sat just behind the front seats. The general still occasionally muttered under his breath. Each time, Bianchi shushed him. When Nate motioned to Don, he nodded and slid behind the wheel.

Nate climbed into the shotgun seat of the van, and Don started the engine. Don pulled from the parking lot onto the road. Settling into his seat, Nate used Don's phone to call the burner phone he and Janelle bought on their way to the ranch. While it rang, he stopped to figure out how long ago that was. *Just over a month?* He shook his head. When Janelle jumped into his SUV, events started in fast forward and didn't show any sign of slowing down anytime soon.

"Hello?"

If someone told him two months ago a woman's soft voice would affect him so much... Nate closed his eyes. For a moment, he couldn't answer. It was so good to hear her voice. "Hello, sweetheart."

"Nate! Where are you?" She sounded as excited to talk to him as he was to talk to her.

"I'm in San Antonio. I'm bringing five extra people to

the ranch with us. At least two will be staying, the others will leave in a day or so. I expect Jackson's son and pack to show up sometime tomorrow. It won't be a friendly visit." Nate glanced at Eli. "We'll be there before supper time. How are things going there?"

"It's been...hard. I'll explain everything when you get here. I'm so happy you're coming home!"

"Are you okay? You sound a little strained."

He heard her sharp breath and frowned. "Janelle, honey..."

"I'm okay. Everything has been resolved. Be safe, Nate."

Nate hesitated, then asked, "Is Jonathan with you?"

"Yes. Do you need to talk with him?"

"Yes. I'll be home in a couple of hours. I love you, Janelle."

"Love you, too. Here's Jonathan."

Nate heard the phone passed from one hand to another.

"Afternoon, Nate." Jonathan's voice held no stress.

Nate relaxed a bit. "Everything okay there?"

"We had some excitement last night, but everything's okay, now. Bradley's dead."

Nate felt the tension spring back into his shoulders. "Dead?"

"Yeah. If you can, you should wait and talk with Janelle about it when you get here."

"She's okay? Nothing wrong with the baby?"

"Janelle and baby are fine. Did you need anything else?"

Nate winced. They were keeping something from him. Sighing, he turned and glanced over his shoulder at Eli where he sat with Renate at the back of the van, then turned his attention back to Jonathan. "Think you could get a half dozen RV's rented and out to the ranch this afternoon?"

"Shouldn't be a problem. Any particular style or model?"

"No, just something comfortable. Rent them for a week." Glancing again at Eli, Nate shrugged. "You know, there's no telling how long we'll need them. Just buy a dozen and move them in. Park them within sight of the main house. Might have some plans drawn up for a storage garage for them, too."

"Will do."

"And Jonathan, we'll be having some unpleasant company sometime tonight or tomorrow. Arm the men until further notice." He swore under his breath. "We really need to get enough weapons to arm the women, too."

*****

While Janelle ran down the stairs, Jonathan followed at a more sedate pace. He grinned at her exuberance, happy something brought her out of her funk. Killing Bradley really got to her.

"Flora!"

Flora stepped out of the kitchen into the hall just as Janelle reached the bottom of the stairs. Janelle grabbed her arms and started bouncing like an excited kid. "Nate's on his way home. He's in San Antonio, so he'll be here soon!"

Jonathan grinned when Flora laughed. "Excited much?"

Janelle laughed with her and nodded. "Yes! Let's get everything ready for steaks and homemade ice cream for supper."

"Sounds good. Did he finish his mission?"

"Must have. He's bringing five extra people with him, so we need to grill more than usual."

Janelle turned to look at Jonathan. "Can you start the grill?"

Jonathan grinned at her and shook his head. "Nate gave me orders, but I'll have Reese do it."

The woman he considered a sister nodded. "Flora and I will start the salad and prepare the potatoes for baking."

"Sounds good. I have to go to Hallettsville for a while, but Ben will be here if you need anything. I'll be taking some of the clowder adults with me, so they can help drive the RVs back."

"RVs?"

"Yeah. Nate wants a dozen here this afternoon." Nodding to the two women, he excused himself and hurried outside. On the porch, he clanged the dinner triangle. When the pack had gathered, he whistled to get their attention.

"Nate will be home in a couple of hours. We may have some unfriendly visitors soon after." He looked at Ben. "Ben, you and the teens arm yourselves. You'll be staying here to protect the ranch. Reese, after you're armed, start the big barbecue pit. We're having steaks tonight."

Reese nodded.

"I need thirteen volunteers with driver's licenses to go with me. Nate wants a dozen RV's purchased and on the ranch by tonight. Anyone who can drive and doesn't have previous assignments this afternoon, move to my left."

Jonathan watched a large group move to his left, some wolves, some panthers, some bears, then counted out thirteen, twelve to drive the RVs and one more in addition to himself to drive back the two SUVs they were taking. He nodded. "The rest of you, arm yourselves." He looked at the thirteen. "We leave in fifteen minutes. Get ready."

As they dispersed, Jonathan reentered the house and headed to the office. After a quick call to the bank to ensure they would authorize such a large withdrawal, he opened the top desk drawer, located the ranch Green Charge Card, and slipped it into his wallet. With no charge limit, it would work, regardless the amount he ended up spending. After a final call to the RV dealer in Hallettsville to ensure they had what he needed, he closed the office door behind him.

Downstairs, he stepped into the kitchen. Janelle and Flora were washing potatoes in preparation for wrapping them in foil for the grill. "I'll be gone a while, Janelle. Need anything from Hallettsville?"

Janelle shook her head. "Everything we need was delivered this morning."

"Okay. Ben has a group patrolling the ranch. If you need anything, let him know."

Janelle grinned over her shoulder at him. "Be careful!"

Jonathan nodded. "Will do."

Exactly fifteen minutes elapsed when the two SUVs pulled out of the compound.

Chapter 20

Sixty foil-wrapped potatoes and four humongous salads later, Janelle looked at the food on the bar and grinned at Flora and Dottie. "Think we have enough?"

Dottie laughed. "Should be plenty. How many ice cream freezers do you think we need to make?"

Janelle wiped her forehead with the back of her right hand. "We have fifteen freezers. Think that will be enough?"

Dottie glanced at Flora. The clowder Queen shrugged. "I don't know. Hope so. Those bears can really put the food away."

Janelle grunted her agreement. "We'll just have to make sure no one gets seconds until everyone has had some."

"That should work." Flora scraped the last of the chopped bell pepper into the fourth salad. "Especially if we dip it, instead of letting everyone dip for themselves."

Nodding, Janelle grabbed the salad tongs and started tossing the veggies in the fourth and final salad. She glanced at the wall clock. "They should be here anytime in the next half hour."

Dottie walked to the restaurant-sized refrigerator. "Let's get the ingredients together for the ice cream, then. Maybe by the time steaks are ready, Jonathan and the others will be back, too." Twenty minutes later, the three women recruited some of the teen girls to carry the prepped ice cream freezers to the warehouse walk-in fridge.

Full of nerves, Janelle started tossing the salads again. A car horn sounded. Janelle dropped the salad tongs into the salad bowl. "They're here!"

She spun and left the kitchen at a run. She hit the front screen door without slowing down. The screen door slammed back against the wall. Before she could get down the steps, Nate was out of the SUV. He caught her against him and lifted her to plant a kiss on her lips, her feet several inches off the ground. Her arms wrapped around his neck, she opened her mouth to him, drowning in the sensations the touch of her mate sent through her.

She was aware several car doors opened, and a group of people emerged from the vehicle, but her attention was all for Nate. When he finally pulled back to let her breathe, she grinned at him. "Welcome home, cowboy."

He laughed, pecked a kiss on her nose, then set her on her feet. "Feels good to be home." His right hand cupped her face. "I missed you."

"Missed you more!"

His smile reached his eyes, caused them to twinkle in the late afternoon sunlight. Steps on the dry dirt behind him caught his attention, and he turned with Janelle. "Janelle, this is Renate Bianchi. She and Eli will be mated tomorrow morning."

Delighted, Janelle grinned. "Welcome, Renate."

Renate briefly bowed her head but didn't speak. Nate motioned toward the others. "You remember the general?"

Janelle nodded. Her grin faded at the angry glance he sent her. "I remember."

"This is Secretary Bianchi, Secretary of Defense, and Renate's father."

"Honored, Secretary."

Nate pointed at the man standing next to the general. "This is Don. He helped us retrieve Renate. She was kidnapped and we went after her." He waved a hand at the last in his party. The scent of unease with a touch of fear hovered around him. "This is Marston. He'll be staying with us for a while."

Marston nodded. Janelle thought the poor man was struggling not to panic. She smiled at him. "Welcome to the Ranch, Marston. If Nate welcomes you, no one here will harm you."

Marston swallowed. "Thank you, ma'am." He shot a frightened look at Nate and ducked his head.

Janelle turned her gaze to Nate. "What happened? What is he so afraid of?"

Nate sighed. "Eli's a bit...overprotective...right now. He keeps growling at Marston."

Janelle blinked, then laughed. Marston looked up, surprise on his face. Janelle squeezed Nate's hand then let go to walk to Marston. She put her hand out to shake his hand. "It'll be easier after the mating."

Nate growled. "Maybe."

Marston snatched his hand back from Janelle, his gaze jumping to Nate. Janelle whipped around. She shook her finger at Nate. "Stop that. You guys have teased him enough."

Nate studied her for a moment, then grinned sheepishly. "Sorry."

"Don't tell me. Tell Marston."

Nate laughed out loud. "You're right." He looked at Marston and grinned at the startled look on his face. "Sorry, Marston. Wolves can be a little harsh in their humor."

Janelle tisked her tongue at Nate and shook her head, then looked at Marston. "Did Nate say you were under his protection?"

Marston nodded.

"Then unless you attack someone on the ranch, you have nothing to be afraid of. Nate won't allow anything to happen to you."

Marston blinked and cut his gaze to Nate.

Nate nodded. "She's right. No one here will hurt you as long as you don't try to hurt anyone."

Janelle smelled the difference when he relaxed a little. She grinned. "What's your first name, Marston?"

"Phillip."

"Well, Phillip, welcome to the ranch." She glanced over the entire group. "We'll have steaks for supper in about an hour."

*****

Tires grated on the road, and multiple engines roared, coming closer to the house. Nate turned and watched a dozen RVs follow two ranch SUVs into the compound. After lining up a short distance from the house, the vehicles stopped. Jonathan jumped out of the first SUV and led the thirteen men and women he took with him to the gathering in front of the main house porch.

"Welcome home, Nate."

"Thanks, Jonathan. Have any trouble with the RVs?"

Jonathan shook his head and laughed. "No. The ranch is now the RV dealership's favorite customer."

Nate grinned. "I imagine so." He glanced at Eli. "Since you don't have a room in the house, Eli, one of those is for you and Renate. I want one for Marston and Don for the night. Another for the general and Secretary Bianchi." He looked at Jonathan. "Reserve two for future guests, and share them out as needed among the bears and others."

"Nate?" Janelle bit her lip, glanced at Jonathan, then turned back to Nate. "We need one for Bradley's widow and family."

Nate frowned at the sharp indrawn breath from Secretary Bianchi. "You mentioned he died."

"He, um, he..." She shuddered and bowed her head.

Nate's frown deepened. "What?"

Jonathan interrupted. "Nate."

Nate kept his gaze on Janelle's flushed face. "Jonathan?"

Jonathan cleared his throat. Nate shifted his gaze from Janelle to Jonathan. Jonathan met his gaze head on. "Bradley attacked Janelle two nights ago. She killed him in self-defense."

A shaft of fear shimmered down Nate's spine. Koreth howled in anger. Nate struggled to keep his wolf under control, the struggle coming out in a harsh tone. "You were supposed to protect her."

Jonathan dropped his gaze, offering his neck to Nate.

"Nate, please."

At Janelle's soft pleading, Nate looked down at her. "We had no reason to believe he would try anything. He waited until everyone was sleeping, then came to my room." She swallowed and shrugged. "When Bradley attacked, I shot him. It's not Jonathan's fault."

Nate searched her face. "You're not hurt?

"Not physically, no. I..." She swallowed and cleared her throat. "I never killed anyone, before, so..."

When tears entered her eyes, Nate pulled her to him. Her arms slipped around him. After a moment, he could ease his grip. "I'm sorry I wasn't here." He felt the stiffness in her body slowly release. She leaned into him. Pressing his cheek against the top of her head, he frowned. Glancing at the people gathered around, he waved his hand.

"Jonathan, assign three RVs to Eli and the men I brought here. Everyone go about your business until the call to supper." He bent and scooped Janelle into his arms, walked up the steps, and carried her inside. When he stepped on the bottom step on the stairs, Janelle moaned.

He looked down at her. "What?"

"I can't go there."

"Our room?"

"Yes." She clenched her eyes tight. "Dusty and Jonathan cleaned it up, but I can't..."

"It's okay." He carried her into the office and sat in his executive's chair, settling her into his lap. He stroked her back and kissed her forehead. "I'll fix it. Paint, new furniture, new curtains, new carpet...whatever you want." He pulled back and looked into her eyes. "It'll be a whole new room. If you prefer, we can move into one of the other houses or have a new one built."

Her sigh was a soft breath against his chest. "As long as you're with me, changing the room should be enough."

Chapter 21

Eli caught Renate's hand in his and turned toward the RVs. Before he took more than two steps, Secretary Bianchi stepped in front of him. Eli stopped and stared at the smaller man.

"You're not taking her in there with you."

Eli raised an eyebrow. "I've already told you she's my mate."

"You aren't mated yet, and she has been promised."

"Dad, stop it. I won't mate Jackson's spawn."

"Renate, you know how powerful the Ozark pack is."

Eli frowned. "Doesn't matter how powerful they are. Renate's mine. Nate..."

"Nate doesn't understand what he's doing." The secretary ran a shaking hand through his hair. "If you go forward, you will be challenged."

"So?"

"So, Sinclair is a powerful, half-royal born-wolf. As a changeling, you don't have a chance."

Renate caught her breath. Eli glanced at her, frowned at the fear on her face, and looked back to Bianchi. "I'm not afraid of Sinclair. Renate is mine. I will protect her."

"You've got the alpha talk down, boy, but you don't have the power. Sinclair is son to Jackson, a Royal Alpha."

Eli shrugged. "Nate is the Alpha King. If he says Renate can make her choice, there's nothing Sinclair can do."

"Fool. Nate can give her a choice, but that won't keep Sinclair from challenge. You won't survive the challenge, and he'll have her, anyway."

"Leave us alone, Dad!" Renate tugged Eli's hand and pulled him away from the crowd. When they got to the picnic shelter, away from everyone, she stopped and faced him.

Eli stroked her face with his right thumb. "Don't be afraid, Renate. I've been training in martial arts since I was just a kid. I can take care of myself."

"But..." She pulled away from the finger he pressed to her lips. "Eli, I have to know something."

"What?"

"You said Nate changed you."

Eli nodded. "Accidentally, when we were kids."

"As a true Royal, he should have one of the medallions."

"He has...several. They melded together when he touched them, but he's had one since before I met him."

Her eyes searched his face. "And you could see it?"

He shrugged. "Didn't notice until..." Eli felt his eyes widen. "Until I got out of the hospital after we had our blood-brother ceremony."

"The one where you shared blood?"

"Yes." Eli frowned. "What are you thinking?"

"I'll tell you in a minute. It's really important that you think hard and be sure you're right in your answer."

"Okay."

"Eli, did you ever touch Nate's medallion?"

Eli snickered. "Yeah. First time I saw it, I reached out and picked it up. Shocked the snot out of me."

"Did you touch it again?"

Eli nodded. "We wanted to see if it would shock me again."

"Did it?"

"No. I felt kind of...weird, like my hand itched to keep it." Eli shook his head. "After that, I didn't try to touch it again. It was Nate's. It was all he had left of his parents. I wouldn't take something that meant so much to him, no matter how much it tempted me."

"But it didn't knock you out?"

"No." When she glanced over her shoulder, Eli thought she was worried her father might have followed them. "Bianchi's still over there with the others. What's wrong?"

"Dad's right, Eli." She put her arms around his neck. Eli let her pull him to her. "I want you, but Sinclair will kill you." She stood on her toes and pressed a kiss to his lips.

Confused, Eli accepted the kiss, then deepened it. He felt her arms slide down his sides until her hands rested on his hips. Her hands slipped into his front pockets. A slow flame filled him, and he pulled her closer. He moaned when she pulled back.

"I'm sorry. I hope I'm right."

Eli frowned at the fear in her eyes. "What?"

"Please, Eli. Just for a moment, close your eyes."

"Why?"

"Please."

Eli shrugged. "Okay." Wondering what she had in mind, he closed his eyes. Her arms brushed his ears. He thought she was putting her arms around his neck, and he pulled her closer.

From the gathering in front of the house, Eli heard Bianchi shout, "Renate, no!"

He opened his eyes just in time to see the chain of the medallion he forgot to return to Bianchi drop over his head. He blinked, then screamed in pain as the suddenly blistering medallion settled against his chest. Clutching at the medallion, he cried out again when the burn speared through his hand.

As if from a long distance, he heard Renate whisper, "I'm so sorry, Eli."

Dropping to his knees, pain racking his entire body, Eli looked up at her. "What did you do?" he whispered. Pain enveloped him. "What did you do?" Consciousness faded. Vaguely he heard her crying, then knew nothing.

Chapter 22

Nate lowered his head to share another kiss with Janelle, ignoring the soft conversations drifting in the open window from the yard. "I missed you," he murmured against her lips.

"I missed you, too." She nibbled his bottom lip. "I love you, Nate."

"Love you, too." He leaned back and gently laid his hand on her stomach. "How's the baby?"

"She's good."

"She?" Nate raised an eyebrow and grinned. "We're having a girl? How do you know?"

"Werewolves always know." She grinned back, her eyes twinkling. "She can't wait to meet her daddy."

"Um, I can't wait to meet her, either." Nate kissed her forehead. "What do you want to name her?"

"I was thinking about Ophelia. It was my mother's name. What do you think?"

"Hmm. Ophelia Linette? My mother's name was Linette."

"I like that." Janelle set her hand on top of Nate's where it rested on her stomach. "What do you think of Ophelia Linette, little one? Like it?"

Nate gasped when the baby moved beneath their hands. Janelle laughed. "I think she likes it, Nate."

Nate chuckled and gently rubbed her stomach. "I think so, too."

"Renate, no!"

Nate jerked upright. "What?"

Eli's scream rent the air. Nate jumped out of his chair,

set Janelle on her feet, then ran out the office door. A moment later, he slammed the front screen door open. Stopping, he visually searched for his brother. Again, Eli shouted in pain. The picnic shelter. Janelle's running steps followed Nate to the shelter.

Eli collapsed on the concrete floor. Renate sat on her knees beside him, tears streaming down her face. When Nate dropped to his knees beside them, she looked at him, fear making her eyes huge.

"What happened, Renate?"

"The medallion." She caught a sobbing breath and pointed toward the medallion laying on Eli's chest.

Nate cursed and reached for it. Before he could touch it, Koreth took control, refusing to allow him to touch it. *You touch it, we die!* "But Eli..." *Eli is a Royal Changeling. He will be okay.* Nate stroked Eli's hair out of his face. *Are you sure?* Nate felt Koreth's affirmation. *He touched your medallion years ago and lived. Your Royal blood protected him, else he would have died then.*

Nate took a moment to control his breathing. *If you're sure...* He looked at Renate. She had her arms wrapped around her waist, and rocked back and forth. "Why did he put it on, Renate?"

Renate sobbed. "He didn't. I put it on him." She recoiled from the anger Nate blasted toward her.

"Why?"

"To keep him alive." She gasped for a breath. "Sinclair will challenge. Without the medallion, Eli won't survive. I can't bear for him to die."

"I told you I would protect you. I gave you a choice."

"Yes, but that wouldn't protect Eli from the challenge. Sinclair is a Royal half-breed. Eli wouldn't survive that kind of power."

"The medallion can kill non-royals."

"I know. Eli told me he could touch yours, so I thought he could wear this one. Without it, he would die in the challenge."

"You had no right..."

Janelle put her arms around Renate. "Nate, that's enough."

Nate frowned at her. "Janelle..."

"What's done is done. It can't be undone any more than you can undo the wearing of your medallion. Scaring Renate to death isn't helping."

Nate's anger flashed again. Janelle winced and jerked back. Realizing he was broadcasting and hurting her, he immediately dropped a shield over his emotions. "I'm sorry, Janelle. It was not intentional."

"I know that. Remember when I told you the anger of a Royal had the force of a weapon?"

Nate nodded. "I remember."

"Keep a lid on it, or there will be more than one person sick tonight." She tilted her head toward the people behind her.

Nate blinked and raised his gaze to sweep the group of wolves, panthers, bears, and humans gathered around him. To a person, they were struggling with pain. Nate caught his breath. Closing his eyes, he centered himself, entering mushin, then opened his shields and let calm flow to his people. When they relaxed and gave a collective sigh of relief, he looked back at Janelle, then at Renate.

Janelle put her hand on his shoulder and he looked up at her. *She believed it was the only way to keep him alive, Nate. If I truly believed the same about you, I would do the same.*

Nate nodded and released the last of the anger he held inside. "As would I for you," he said aloud.

Eli moaned. Nate leaned over him, lightly slapped his face. "Wake up, Eli."

After another moan, Eli's eyelids fluttered, then opened. He looked up into Nate's eyes and whispered, "I'm sorry, Nate."

Nate shook his head. "Nothing to be sorry about. Can you get up?"

Eli shuddered, then nodded. "I think so."

Nate slipped his arm under his brother's shoulders and helped him to sit. "Feel any better?"

"Have a mother of a headache, but I don't hurt anywhere else, now."

"Maybe some aspirin will help. Let's get you in the house. You should probably lay down for a little while."

"Eli..."

Eli looked at Renate. "Oh, baby..." He opened his arms. "It's okay."

Renate fell against him, her tears wetting his shoulder. "I'm sorry. I couldn't risk losing you."

Eli stroked her hair and sighed. "It's okay, sweetheart."

Nate watched in silence. He glanced at Janelle. She was watching Eli and Renate. The calming balm of Koreth's reassurance settled him. *Eli is okay, Nate.*

Secretary Bianchi pushed through the crowd. "Renate, how could you?"

In answer, she buried her face against Eli. When the secretary reached to grab her shoulder, Nate intercepted him, his big hand wrapping around the secretary's wrist. "Enough, Secretary. As Janelle said, done is done."

"But that medallion belongs to my family."

Renate sniffed. "It belongs to the man I mate," she said into Eli's chest.

Nate frowned. "Is that true, Secretary?"

"Well, it was to go to her mate, but Sinclair..."

"Eli is her mate. The medallion accepted him. It belongs to him, now." Nate pulled the secretary two steps from Renate and Eli. "Get this through your head. As Royal Alpha and Council Alpha, I sanction their union. Sinclair can challenge if he wants to, that's pack law. I've trained with Eli for years. Even without the medallion, Eli had a good chance to win. With it, Sinclair should think again."

Bianchi pressed his lips tight, his gaze moving from Nate to Eli. After a glance at Renate, his expression softened. He dropped his shoulders and bowed his head. Eli stood up and pulled Renate with him. Nate stepped aside to allow his brother access to the secretary.

"Secretary Bianchi, I know you don't know me, but I will protect Renate with my life for the rest of my life."

Nate watched, silent, as Bianchi seemed to fight with himself, then the secretary sighed and nodded. He frowned at Eli. "Since you are the mate Renate wants, and since the medallion accepted you, I will accept you, too." He cast a look at Nate, then looked back at Eli. "However, under pack law, it will make your claim stronger if you are mated." Bianchi swallowed then shrugged. "I suggest you mate tonight. Before Sinclair arrives."

Renate gasped. Nate laughed at the stunned look on Eli's face. He clapped his hand on Eli's shoulder. "If you'll all excuse us, I think I need to chat with Eli for an hour or so." He grinned at Janelle and nodded toward Renate. "Help her get ready?"

Delight on her face, Janelle clapped her hands and

nodded. "Of course. We can celebrate with steaks and ice cream after!"

"Then I'll take this brother of mine in hand and make sure he knows what he's gotten himself into." Nate pulled an unresisting Eli into the house and up the stairs. After closing the office door behind them, Nate motioned toward an empty chair. "Sit down, Eli. You won't believe what I'm going to tell you, but I promise it's all true."

Chapter 23

Don stood on the grass twenty feet from the two-story gazebo. The sun set on the horizon, sending its golden light, the last rays of the day, across the ranch. Phillip Marston seemed to feel as lost among the *were* as Don did. Phillip seldom left Don's side, as if there was safety for humans in numbers. Don glanced around at the number and size of the *were* and shook his head. *If things go south, we're both goners. There's no way we can fight through this crowd.*

Deciding to trust Nate's word that no one would harm them, Don sighed, twisted his right arm up his back and scratched an itch he could barely reach. Eli held Renate's hand and walked up the steps to the top of the gazebo. Eli turned and faced Renate. The two of them whispered too low for Don to hear. Then, Eli spoke one word out loud, almost in a growl. "Mine!"

Even though Don saw Eli shift into a wolf before, it surprised him when only Eli's face shifted into a wolf. Eli moved the fabric on Renate's shoulder to the side, sank his teeth into her shoulder, then licked the blood that welled from the bite. His face became human again. Fascinated, but at the same time wishing he could look away, Don watched Renate's nose elongate into a wolf's snout. She pushed the neck of Eli's t-shirt to the side, baring his shoulder, bit him, and then licked away the blood that welled from Eli's wound.

They kissed, then shifted into wolves. Eli's wolf claimed her, howling as he did. The *were* around Don suddenly shifted, too, their howls, yowls, and growls blending in celebration with Eli's. Wide-eyed, Don turned his head and scanned the *were* around him. Bears, wolves, and panthers joined in the celebration. Only Don, Phillip, and the general remained as humans. Marine Ranger though he was, Don swallowed. He felt Phillip's panic when the other man's left hand caught the back of Don's shirt in a tight-fisted grip. Don ignored him.

As suddenly as the howling started, it stopped. Bears, wolves, and panthers shimmered into humans. Nate waved his hands, dismissing the crowd. Quietly, the *were* walked away. Don swallowed but met Nate's gaze without flinching. Nate nodded at him. "Let's go to the house. I'm sure Janelle has some tea made."

Without a word, Don followed Nate and Janelle to the house, peripherally aware the general and secretary went with them. Phillip still had hold of Don's shirt. Don twitched in irritation and pulled the fabric from Phillip's hand. Phillip blinked then gave Don a sheepish grin.

"Sorry about that."

Don nodded. "No problem." He glanced over his shoulder to the gazebo where the two wolves consummated their union. He blew out a breath and shook his head. *Just what did the general get me into?*

Don walked into the kitchen and sat on the bar stool Nate pointed at, Phillip taking the stool beside him. The secretary snagged another stool and seemed lost in thought. Refusing to sit, the general's sour expression and huffs ensured even the two humans were aware he was not happy.

Janelle pulled out glasses. Nate used the ice dispenser on the refrigerator door to fill them. As he set each glass on the bar, Janelle poured southern sweet tea over the ice, then handed one to each of the men. Don glanced around, a bit surprised no one else came to the kitchen with them.

After they all had a glass of tea, Nate raised his glass in the air. "Cheers, gentlemen." He grinned and looked down at Janelle. "And lady, of course."

Janelle smiled at him. "We need to get the steaks started soon. The charcoal is probably starting to die down."

Nate nodded and picked up the walkie-talkie sitting on the end of the bar. After he contacted Jonathan, he gave orders to refresh the charcoal and get the picnic shelter ready for the evening meal. Janelle put a hand on his arm. Nate raised an eyebrow at her.

"Tell Jonathan we put ice cream freezers in the warehouse walk-in fridge. The boys need to start cranking them while the steaks cook."

Nate snickered. "Ice cream? Thinking of Eli?"

Janelle laughed and slapped his arm. "No, silly, you're the one who likes ice cream." She shook her finger at him. "No punching Eli on his mating day." Nate laughed.

Don exchanged glances with Phillip and shrugged. "Inside joke, maybe?"

Nate laughed again. "Yeah, it is. Sorry about that." He frowned and looked at the secretary. "Something eating you, Secretary?"

Bianchi raised his head. Worry in his expression, he nodded. Don was surprised when the secretary's eyes cut toward him and Phillip. "Not sure I can ask right now."

Nate shrugged. "They know most of our secrets now, anyway. What is it?"

Don frowned when the Secretary swallowed, and he realized the man was afraid.

"Eli is a Royal Changeling?"

Nate nodded. "He is. If he wasn't, he'd be dead. The

medallion won't allow anyone without Royal blood to wear it."

"Um, so, just how Royal is he?"

"Pardon?"

"I mean, when a true Royal wears the medallion, he becomes..." The secretary swallowed.

Fascinated, Don watched the emotions playing over Nate's face. Apprehension rolled off Nate in waves. Don frowned and shivered. *Didn't Janelle say something about Nate broadcasting emotions?*

Janelle put her hand on Nate's. Slowly, the apprehension faded. Nate looked down at her. "Do you suppose…?"

"I don't know, Nate. You trust him, don't you?"

Watching the silent strain between them, Don pursed his lips.

Nate nodded. "I do trust him. More than I trust anyone other than you."

"Then it doesn't matter." Janelle turned to the secretary. "Secretary Bianchi, Nate and Eli have been true blood brothers since they were kids. Eli is one of the good guys, through and through. You don't have to worry."

Don watched Secretary Bianchi study Janelle's sincere eyes, then look at Nate. "And if he turns traitor?"

"He won't." Nate shrugged. "Even if he's Lycos, he won't betray me. He's my brother."

Already confused, Don struggled to understand. "What's a Lycos?"

Everyone ignored him as if he hadn't spoken.

"Jackson was your father's twin brother. He had your father killed, and tried to kill you," Bianchi said, his tone flat.

The general moved closer to Don. "Suppose we make sure about Eli?"

Nate's frown deepened. "And how do you propose we do that?"

"As Council Alpha, you could force him to tell you if he is."

Nate glared at the general. Don swallowed, relieved the anger wasn't directed at him. "General," Nate set his tea glass on the bar. "Eli is...Eli. I know you don't know what that means, but I give you my word, Eli is not dangerous to us. Any of us."

A strained silence hovered, then the general nodded, doubt in his expression. "And you, Rollins? Are you dangerous to us?"

Nate sneered. The blue light that glowed around Nate when Eli removed the bullet from Renate's shoulder suddenly outlined Nate. "Only occasionally, General. Only occasionally."

General Brighton staggered back, his face betraying his fright. Don's gaze flitted from the general to the secretary, and back to Nate. There were undercurrents he couldn't grasp. Suddenly, not for the first time, he wished he was somewhere else. Anywhere else.

Chapter 24

Morning light filtered through the opaque white curtains draped over the RV's small windows, shutting out the bright morning sun. Eli smiled down at Renate. Her long brown hair fanned across the pillow beneath her head. Brushing strands of her hair from her shoulder, he bent and pressed a kiss to the faint scar from his mating bite. She opened her eyes and looked at him.

Eli kissed her shoulder again. "Good morning, beautiful."

"Good morning." Turning toward him, she molded herself to him, her head on his arm. Concern touched her face. "Are you okay?"

"I'm better than okay." Eli grinned. "We don't have to get up, yet."

She smiled and slipped her arm around his waist. "Then let's don't."

Her kiss pulled him closer to her. Rolling with her, his weight pressing her into the mattress, he kissed her nose. His voice more growl than words, he said, "I like the way you think, mate."

She laughed. Her arms circled his neck and pulled him into a deep, soul-burning kiss. The kind of kiss that meant more.

*****

In the main house kitchen, Renate helped Janelle and Flora prepare pancakes for a crowd. She looked at the five large roasting pans overflowing with pancakes and shook her head. "You don't think it's too much?"

Janelle shook her head. "Nope. Without the bears and their families, the pack could easily consume two pans full. The bears really like to chow down, so we'll need this much. I just hope we have enough."

Renate quirked her mouth. "Maybe so. It just seems like a lot."

Flora set two buckets filled with syrup and honey bottles on the counter. "There won't be any left. Like Janelle said, those bears really eat." She grinned. "They won't quit until there's nothing left. And the rest of us like to eat, too."

Renate grinned. "A hazard of being *were*, I suppose."

"Yep. Good thing we don't have to watch our weight." Janelle turned to add paper plates, napkins, and plastic ware to another bucket. She caught her breath and gripped the edge of the counter.

Flora was instantly at her side. "What's wrong?"

Janelle took a slow breath and shook her head. "Nothing. Ophelia's kicks are getting stronger."

Renate and Flora exchanged glances and grinned. Renate sat on a stool. "When are you due?"

Janelle blew out a breath of relief, then holding her stomach, she eased onto a stool. "The middle of June."

Flora fluttered around her like Janelle was her very own kitten. "Need anything?"

"No." Janelle grinned. "Sit down for a minute, Flora. You're making me nervous."

Flora dropped to a third stool. "You sure you don't need anything?"

Janelle laughed and patted her friend's shoulder. "I'm fine. Calm down or you'll have Nate barging in here."

Flora snickered. “He’s a worse mother hen than I am.”

“He is.” Janelle smiled at Renate. “How is Eli today?”

Renate basked in the warmth of Janelle’s smile and returned it with one of her own. “He’s okay.” She felt her smile slip. When she forced it back on her face, she realized the other two women would see how brittle it was. “I was so scared.”

Janelle handed her a cup of coffee. “You really didn’t think Eli could win against Sinclair?”

Renate swallowed. “Sinclair is worse than his father was. He’s a killer and he enjoys it.” She tried to ease the strain in her shoulders. “Jackson raised him that way. The only one who ever had any control over him was Jackson.”

Memories of the summer Renate spent in Jackson’s pack filled her mind. She shuddered. “More than once, I saw Jackson backhand Sinclair to prevent him from killing someone Jackson wanted alive. Now that Jackson’s dead, I don’t think Sinclair will accept anyone telling him he can’t have what he wants.”

“So, you really thought he would kill Eli.” Janelle’s soft statement brought Renate’s eyes to her.

“Yes. He will try.” She swallowed. “I thought the medallion was Eli’s only chance for survival. I...I couldn’t bear it if Sinclair killed him.” Blinking away tears, she looked down at her coffee cup. “Eli’s my mate. Sinclair would have me to kill, too, if he killed Eli.”

*****

Nate studied the men sitting in the picnic shelter. The bears had joined the male wolves and panthers in his pack for this meeting. “Sinclair will be here sometime this morning. I don't know who or how many he'll bring with him. Bianchi..." He nodded toward Eli's father-in-law. "Bianchi thinks he'll come in force. For the time being, those of you who have weapons, continue to wear them. Don't use them unless one of us..." Nate indicated Jonathan, Dusty, Ben, and Eli. "Unless one of us gives the order."

He looked at the bear's leader, the former execution squad leader and frowned. "You know, I don't think you ever told me your name."

The bear smiled. "You never asked Alpha. It's Daryll. Daryll Crane."

"Crane?"

Daryll laughed. "Several centuries ago, when my great-great grandfather was just a cub, he brought crane home for lunch. The den thought it was funny to try to feed everyone with just one bird, so he was called Crane after that. The name stuck and eventually became the family name."

Nate grinned. "That explains it." He jerked his chin toward the rest of the bears. "You still in charge of the bears?"

"Unless you decide otherwise, Alpha."

"Nope. I can't do everything. Jonathan is in charge of the wolves, and Will helps Flora with the panthers. You seem to be doing a good job, so you can keep it."

Crane nodded. "Thank you."

Nate looked at the other bears to make sure no one had complaints. When none arose, he looked at Crane. "Mind being enforcers for a bit longer? Not executioners, just enforcers. I won't require it of you since Jackson forced you into the role against your will."

"Alpha, the difference between you and Jackson makes

all the difference we need. If you want enforcers, we are happy to be enforcers for you." The other bears nodded agreement.

Nate blew out a loud breath. "Thanks. That helps. While Sinclair and his bunch are here, I want you to keep them in line. Don't worry about Sinclair. I'll take care of him if he tries to cause trouble beyond the challenge, but I can't be everywhere, and I want the women and children protected."

Crane bowed his head. "As you command, Alpha."

Irritation edged into Nate's awareness. Sighing, he forced it back. *It's not their fault the were system is a monocracy.* Nate looked at Eli. "Think you're ready?"

Eli's brown eyes hid the humor Nate could feel coming from Eli. "I'm ready."

"Just don't get cocky. Even with the medallion, you could lose, if you aren't careful."

"I'll be careful."

Nate sucked air through his teeth and nodded. "Good." He sniffed and looked toward the house. Several women walked with Janelle toward the shelter, carrying five huge pans of pancakes and buckets full of all the trimmings. He grinned when he saw the bears perk up and start sniffing the air. "Looks like this meeting is over, boys. Breakfast is on the way."

Chapter 25

Nate sipped his coffee, watching the animated conversations of those gathered in the picnic shelter for breakfast. Sporadic laughter sounded through the crowd. A shadow fell across the table, and he looked up. Janelle held the hand of a woman who looked about Janelle's age, but Nate knew his human-trained eye was unable to accurately judge werewolf ages. Behind them, he saw a teen, his chin jutting in defiance, and a set of elementary-aged blonde twin girls.

"Nate, this is Nettie and her family. I mentioned them to you."

Nate raised an eyebrow. "Who...?"

"Nettie is Bradley's widow."

Nate felt his jaw tighten. Before he spoke, Janelle shook her head. "She has asked to join the pack. I have given provisional permission, pending your approval." Janelle must have felt his disquiet. She communicated with him mind-to-mind. *Nate, Bradley abused Nettie and the children. No one would help her when Bradley forced himself on the girls. Jackson permitted his perversion.*

Nate blinked. Both his eyebrows climbed his forehead. When he looked again at Nettie, his reservations vanished. He studied her, noting that she trembled while wringing her hands in the air at her waist. She looked much too young to be the mother of the teen and the girls hiding behind her, peering around at him, their eyes wide. Though he didn't speak, the boy's hostility and anger flared when Nate looked at him.

Koreth pushed at the boy, then told Nate the teen was

afraid Nate would deny them. He was trying to be brave, but in his dread, his fear came across as belligerence. Nate smoothed out his face and spoke to the boy. "What's your name?"

"Trey."

"You ready to stand as the defender of your mother and sisters, Trey?"

Trey stood straighter and lost the rebellion in his stance. "I am."

Nettie's soft voice was almost too quiet to hear. "Alpha?"

Nate looked at Nettie and waited for her to speak. Janelle nodded at her, encouraging her to continue. "It's okay, Nettie. Go ahead."

Nettie swallowed. "With your permission, if you give us leave to stay, I would like to change our name. For my family's healing, and to distance ourselves from Trent's evil."

Surprised at the request, Nate considered her. "What name would you use?"

"My father's name was Dietrich. He died before Jackson gave me to Bradley." She glanced at Janelle, swallowed again, and looked at Nate. "With your permission, we would use my father's name."

Nate grew very still. His anger crashed through the crowd. As one, everyone stopped talking and turned to see what upset the Alpha. "Jackson 'gave' you to Bradley?"

Confusion on her face, Nettie bowed her head. "Yes, Alpha."

Nate took several agitated breaths, then stood up. His gaze raked the crowd. Using the form of speech supplied by Koreth, he spoke, his words carrying the force of Alpha command. "Hear me, pack. This is my command. No female is to be given as mate or forced to mate without her approval. Any may come to me for redress if this command is broken. Hear ye well."

Nate swept his gaze over the crowd. Only the general, Don, and Marston had their heads up. The vampire and two humans looked stunned. Everyone else bowed. Nate ignored the three. "Hear ye well."

The voices of the pack rose in traditional words of obedience. "The Alpha speaks. We obey."

Nate turned back to Nettie. "From this moment, your name is Dietrich. You will not be addressed as or referred to by Bradley's name again. Your petition to join the pack is approved. Welcome."

For a moment, Nate thought she would cry. Blinking, she gave him a tremulous smile. "Thank you, Alpha."

Nate nodded. "You are welcome." He looked at Trey. "When training begins again tomorrow, join the others. Do you know Reese and Adrian?"

Trey nodded. He looked stunned with the adoption. "Yes, Alpha. We've met."

"Good." Nate leaned to the side to see the two girls better. He smiled and crooked his finger at them. Embarrassed at the attention, their faces reddened. When their mother motioned for them to come forward, the two stepped in front of her. Nate leaned over. "What do you like to do? Draw, maybe?"

One of the girls had her thumb in her mouth. The other grinned and nodded. "I like to draw. Mattie likes to paint."

Nate grinned back at her. He pointed at Dottie. "See that nice lady?"

They both nodded. "She has a special play area set up in the back of the main house where all the kids can have fun. She keeps crayons, pencils, and pens, as well as finger paints in there, and lots of other fun stuff. Would you like to see it?"

Both girls nodded. Nate smiled. He stood up. "Her name is Miss Dottie. If you go talk to her, I'm sure she can find you what you need to draw and paint."

Mattie removed her thumb and smiled at him. "Thank you, Alpha."

"You're welcome. You can call me Nate."

"Thank you, Nate." Mattie grinned, displaying her missing front tooth. "I like you."

Nate laughed and winked at Janelle, before bending over again to the girl's height. "I like you, too," he said in a loud stage whisper, "but Janelle gets kind of jealous, so let's don't tell her." He wrinkled his nose at her and winked.

The little girl's eyes grew large. She looked up at Janelle. Over the child's head, Nate grinned at Janelle and saw her school her face into a pretend frown. "Are you flirting with my mate?"

When the girl looked frightened and shook her head, Janelle grinned. "Well, that's okay, then. Want to go see Miss Dottie, now?" She laughed when both girls nodded.

"Let's go." Janelle took each by the hand and walked them toward Dottie.

Nettie smiled. "Thank you, Al...um...Nate."

Nate nodded. "I'm sorry for all you've gone through. I can't change what happened, but it won't happen again." He glanced past her and saw Dusty's interest. "Have you met Dusty?"

"No, Sir."

Nate motioned for Dusty to join them. In the background, the pack once again started talking. When Dusty stepped up to him, Nate raised an eyebrow. "Dusty, would you help Nettie get her family settled in? We'll put her in the house by the pond as soon as it's set up. Until, then, please make sure she has what she needs for her family."

Dusty nodded. "Be happy to." He turned to Nettie. "If you'll come with me, ma'am, you can tell me what your family needs, and I'll see if I can take care of it."

She nodded, smiled at Nate and left with Dusty. With her at his side, Dusty stood a little straighter, carried himself with a little more pride. Nate grinned at them, then glanced at Trey. The boy watched his mother walk away with Dusty. He looked back at Nate. "What you said. You won't give her away, will you?"

Nate looked at the boy and reminded himself what the small family had suffered. "If your mother decides to mate someone, I won't stand in her way, but I will not give anyone to someone else. As far as I'm concerned, that's no different than slavery, and I won't abide it."

The left corner of Trey's mouth twitched, almost grinned. "I think I like you, too, Nate. Janelle doesn't have to be jealous, though." His grin broke through. "I like girls."

Nate laughed. "Go find Reese and get the schedule for training exercises. All the teens are required to attend them."

"Yes, Sir." Trey grinned and walked away.

Chapter 26

Nate stood in front of the main house, with Janelle standing beside him. They faced the six-car convoy that rolled to a stop on the circle drive. The last time outsiders showed up, the bears were with them. This time, they lined up in front of the pack as guards.

Another werebear wearing a chauffeur's uniform opened the back door of a black limousine. A tall man who vaguely resembled Nate stepped out and strutted toward Nate's pack. The group of personal guards and thugs he brought with him fell in behind him. Nate wondered if their visitor could identify him as Alpha, then realized he could when he ignored everyone else and walked to Nate.

"You are?"

The superior tones in the man's voice irked Nate. "You are?"

Eyes narrowed in annoyance, the man brushed nonexistent lint off his suit jacket. "I am Sinclair, Alpha to the Arkansas pack." Bringing his haughty gaze back to Nate, he frowned. "And you are?"

"I'm Nate. Alpha to the Texas pack. What do you want?"

"I'm here for my mate, and to avenge my father's death. I assume you are his killer."

"We fought." Nate crossed his arms. "It was almost a fair fight, too." Nate smirked. "I didn't cheat." Sinclair caught his breath. Nate grinned at his piercing stare. "Do you cheat like your dad did?" Nate knew he was goading the other man, but if he could force him to challenge him rather than Eli, he would.

"Don't push, little man. I am heir to the Arkansas pack and heir to the Council Alpha position."

"Maybe you are heir to the Arkansas pack." Nate shrugged. "That's between you and them. You are not Council Alpha. That position belongs to me."

The song of Texas katydids was suddenly loud in the quiet. Nate returned Sinclair's threatening stare. Sinclair smirked. "That is a battle for another time. Where is my mate?"

"You don't have a mate here."

Nate's cousin's expression grew hard. He glanced past Nate to Secretary Bianchi. "Where is Renate?"

"Renate is already mated to another. Go home."

Fury washed across Sinclair's face. "You agreed to terms!"

"I was forced to agree to your terms to protect the rest of the pack. The Alpha here dissolved the agreement. Renate is mated to another. You're too late."

"I challenge!" Spittle flew with the shouted words.

Nate raised a hand and wiped it off his face with a flick of his thumb. "Eli, Sinclair challenges. Do you accept challenge?"

Eli stepped up beside Nate. "Renate's mine. I accept."

Sinclair took a threatening step toward Eli. Nate stepped between them. "My pack. My territory. My rules."

"Rules?'

"The fight will be in the field. I will officiate. The fight is over when I call it. If either party breaks the rules, you will face me."

Sinclair snarled. "The fight is over when he dies and Renate is mine."

"Understand this, Sinclair. By Pack Law, I can't

prevent this fight, but win or lose, Renate stays here. You can't have her."

"Who do you think you are? No one orders me around. I am of Royal descent."

"I am Nate Rollins, called the missing Royal child, son of your father's twin, Grant. Tread lightly, Sinclair. I already don't like you."

*****

Eli snickered at the rage on Sinclair's face when Nate told him he couldn't have Renate, regardless of the outcome of their fight. He laughed out loud at the fear that leaped into Sinclair's eyes when Nate introduced himself. Not that it lasted long. Sinclair was good at hiding his emotions.

The fear disappeared and the haughty sneer returned. "I'll deal with you later." He glared at Eli. "Where is this field?"

Nate motioned to the grassy field on the other side of the parked cars. "There." He glanced at the men with Sinclair. "Your men will stay here with my enforcers." He motioned to the werebears behind him.

Sinclair growled at them. "You belong to me!"

Crane stepped forward. "We belong to ourselves. Nate is our Alpha. We do not answer to you." He snarled. "Any who wish to leave you and join us will be accepted."

Sinclair blinked. For a moment, the spoiled child showed through. "You can't do that. You belong to me."

"So, I adopted them." Nate's negligent shrug brought a grin to Eli's lips. "Deal with it."

Sinclair huffed. "Maybe I'll just call in reinforcements and flatten your little, decimated pack."

When Nate clenched his fists and stepped forward, Eli touched his shoulder. "Let me. It's my mate he plans to steal."

After a second, Nate nodded. "You challenged, and Eli accepted. Fight or forfeit."

In answer, Sinclair stomped to his car. Once there, he shrugged out of his expensive suit coat, removed his tie and cuff links, and handed them all to his bear chauffeur. The bear took his things, then looked past him to Crane, a worried look on his face.

Sinclair stomped around the car and headed for the field, rolling his sleeves. Nate nodded at Crane. "Allow only five to come to witness the proceedings. The rest are to stay here. Renate, Janelle, Bianchi, Dusty, we will be the witnesses for Eli."

They followed Eli to the field. Sinclair's five witnesses lined the fence on the left side of the gate, while Nate and his group lined the fence on the right. Eli stopped to give Renate a quick kiss, then walked through the gate and faced Sinclair.

Sinclair's eyes were hot red, anger at the kiss Eli gave Renate stirring him up. "You are going to die, wolf."

Eli shrugged. "Maybe. Probably not."

Shouting in rage, Sinclair jumped at Eli, shifting to wolf in mid-air. Before he reached his target, Eli shifted and leaped to meet him. The two crashed together, amid snarls and growls. Grappling, they rolled across the ground. Eli forced Sinclair's teeth away from his neck and lunged, trying to close his massive jaws on Sinclair's neck. Because Eli was human until recently, he didn't have the years of experience fighting in wolf form Sinclair had. Realizing he couldn't beat Sinclair as wolf, Eli rolled away and shifted, crouched low, balancing on the balls of his feet. Sinclair surged toward him. Eli spun and kicked Sinclair's snout.

The wolf howled and yelped in pain. Falling to the ground, Sinclair swiped at his nose with his paw and shook his head. Growling, he jumped to his feet. Before he could close, Eli kicked him again. His spin carried him completely around. Another kick thudded into Sinclair's ribs. The Alpha sprawled. Eli followed, delivering another kick, then another.

Unable to defend against Eli's attack, Sinclair rolled away and shifted. The man held an arm against his ribs, staggering back away from Eli. Eli motioned for the Alpha to come after him. "What's the matter, Sinclair? Too much for you?"

Shouting in rage, Sinclair closed in on Eli. Both men pounded each other. Sinclair tripped Eli. Eli snagged his shirt and pulled the Alpha down with him. They rolled in the dirt, fists pounding bruising blows. Eli forced Sinclair to his back.

Straddling Sinclair's chest, Eli slammed his fist into Sinclair's face. Sinclair tried to unseat Eli, but couldn't. Blow after blow rained down on Sinclair's face until the Alpha was barely conscious.

"Enough!"

Eli barely heard Nate's shout. Jabril pushed into Eli's anger haze, forced him to stop. *The Alpha commands!* Eli rolled away from Sinclair and to his feet. He glared down at Sinclair. "Renate is mine! You touch her, you die!"

Sinclair whimpered. Satisfied Sinclair understood, Eli stretched sore muscles, gasping at the pain in his ribs. He staggered toward the gate. When he heard Renate's growl, he looked up. His eyes grew wide as Renate shifted and leaped over the fence. Eli turned to watch as she charged past him.

Just as she jumped and closed her jaws on Sinclair's throat, Eli saw the knife Sinclair threw at him. Saw it, but did not have time to avoid it. As Sinclair screamed his death cry, the silver blade buried in Eli's chest.

Eli dropped to his knees and looked down at the knife handle protruding from his chest. Renate dropped to her knees beside him, Sinclair's blood on her face and blouse. She reached for the knife and cried out in rage when the silver burned her fingers. "Eli!"

Eli stared at the blade handle, then looked up at her and smiled. "Guess you didn't need a knight on a white horse, after all." Eli fell forward. He felt her catch him before he fell on the knife, causing even more injury. Annoyed with himself for nearly passing out again, he forced himself to keep his eyes open and leaned back.

Jabril pushed forward in his mind, chanting words Eli had never heard. He felt power gather in his chest. Felt the knife inching out. Blinking, he watched as it finally dropped from his wound into the dirt. His blood gushed, then stopped. Power unlike any he had ever felt encompassed him.

Renate reached for him, but stopped, her fingers a few inches short of touching him. "Eli?"

Unable to respond, he cried out and staggered to his feet. Eli threw his head back and roared. He felt himself changing. The change confused him. Rather than shrinking into a wolf, he grew larger, taller, broader.

A blue glow surrounded him, then just as it started to dissipate, he heard a rip. Astonished, he looked over his shoulder at the tail that tore through his jeans. Eli looked at

Nate and swallowed. "I think I ripped my pants."

Chapter 27

Even the katydids stopped singing. In the utter silence following Eli's comment, Nate put a hand on the fence post in front of him. Vaulting over the fence, he walked toward Eli. Renate, misunderstanding his approach, shrank from him, whimpering.

Eli, still in his Lycos form, stepped in front of Renate, his eyes narrowing. "You will not harm my mate."

Nate stopped. "Shift, Eli."

Eli roared and pushed off the compulsion. Nate threw his head back and called his own Lycos form, remembering to phase his pants. He brought his head down and frowned at his brother. "Shift, Eli."

"You will not harm my mate."

Nate glared at Eli. "I will not harm your mate. Shift!" A powerful roar followed the word.

Eli blinked, startled as his form shifted, quickly shrinking back to human. As soon as Eli was human, Nate shifted. Eli swallowed. Nate raised his eyebrow. "Do you really think I would hurt your mate? You're my brother."

"She was frightened."

Nate nodded. "I know, but there was no need for her to be. She defended her mate. I won't punish her for that."

Eli searched his face. Finally convinced, he reached behind him and caught Renate's hand, then pulled her up beside him. Eli blinked, then looked at Nate. "What happened, Nate? You're Lycos, not me."

"Lycos is a form that Royal blood can call when wearing the medallion, Eli. Because my blood changed you, you're a Royal, at least partly so." Nate rubbed at the knots in his neck. "But, Eli, I am a full Royal by birth. That means I will always be more powerful. Even without the extra medallions, that would be true."

"You're welcome to it. That much power..." Eli shivered, cleared his throat, and looked down at Renate. "Are you okay?"

She swallowed and nodded. "I am, now." Renate touched his chest. "Are you okay? The knife..."

Eli looked down at his chest. A narrow scar lined his chest where the solid silver knife struck him. As he watched, the scar shimmered and disappeared. Eli raised his right hand and touched the smooth skin on his chest. He shrugged at the question in Renate's face. "I don't know, either. Jabril took over, started chanting something, then the knife just backed out."

Nate put his hand on Eli's shoulder. "It's time to end this." Eli nodded.

Nate shifted to wolf. Koreth stood on his hind legs, turned and held his paws toward Sinclair. "As from the beginning, as unto the end." Blue flames engulfed Sinclair. Moments later, ash from Sinclair's cremated body settled to the ground.

When the flames shimmered and flickered out, Koreth slammed his massive clawed paws together, sending a roll of thunder across the ranch. "Now from the end, return to the beginning." His paws swept toward the wooded hills. The ashes swirled into the air and were drawn high above the trees beyond the field. The wind funnel carrying them dissipated, and the ashes fell, sifting to disperse over the trees.

Together, the brothers, Renate's hand still in Eli's, turned back to face the *were* standing at the fence. All the *were*, except Janelle, dropped to their knees. Even the general knelt. The two humans standing on the porch looked around, confusion obvious in their faces. Eli looked over the yard, his gaze taking in all the bowing *were*, then looked at Nate. He swallowed. "Does it get easier?"

Nate sighed and shook his head. "Never."

*****

Nate sent the children and some of the women to the play room, then ordered Sinclair's retinue to sit at the tables in the picnic shelter. His pack stood around the shelter, cutting Sinclair's people off from escape, even were they of a mind to try. Nate walked to the head of the shelter and turned to face them. All their heads were bowed, waiting for his instructions.

"Who oversees Sinclair's group?"

At Nate's question, they turned their heads side to side, looking at each other without lifting their heads. Nate sighed. He looked across the shelter and searched until he found Crane. "Crane, come here."

Crane marched to the head of the shelter. "Sire?"

Nate's left eyebrow jerked toward his hairline. "Don't call me that."

"Yes, Sir."

Nate sighed and shook his head. Seemed like that was all he did anymore. Sigh. "Who is the person in charge of this group?"

Crane looked at the men, then pointed at a bear about half-way down the center row. "That's Carson. He's probably in charge."

Nate nodded. "Thanks. Carson, get up here."

Unwilling steps brought Carson to the front. "Sir?"

"This was Jackson's pack."

"Yes, Sir."

Nate glanced at Crane. "Is he trustworthy?"

Crane frowned, considered the question, then nodded. "I think so, Sir." He shrugged. "Most of the pack members were victims of both Jackson and Sinclair. Very few partook of their evil."

Nate nodded. "Of those who 'partook of their evil,' are any here?"

Crane turned to study each of Sinclair's pack members. "Only Berkley."

"Berkley, come up here."

Steps even slower than Carson's, Berkley walked to the front. When he arrived, Nate looked at him, then released Koreth. Koreth invaded Berkley's mind, sifting through it for information. Berkley cried out and dropped to his knees. *Guilty.*

Nate sighed. Again. There had been enough death today. "Berkley, you have been judged and found guilty. You are stripped of pack rights and banished. You will not return to your pack. If you harm anyone, *were* or human, your ability to shift will wither away. You will live out your life as wolf only. If you encroach on any pack territory, your life is forfeit. Any pack may destroy you on sight if you are on their lands. In one hundred years, you may return to a pack and request reprieve. There is none until then." Nate put his hand on Berkley's head. "So be it." Koreth impressed on his mind the punishment Nate decreed. "Leave and do not return."

Sobbing, the man staggered to his feet. Hiding his face from his former compatriots, he walked until he got past

Nate's pack, then shifted and ran as if Nate had tied a burning rag to his tail.

Nate waited until the others turned to look at him again. "Koreth will walk among your thoughts. If you are innocent, you will be released to return to your pack and family. If not, you will receive the same fate as Berkley."

The men bowed their heads and waited as Koreth judged them guilty or innocent. Once Koreth pronounced them innocent of Jackson's and Sinclair's crimes, Nate cleared his throat. "Until I give you permission, you will remain here." He looked at his pack. "Return to your duties."

His pack moved away. Nate looked at Eli. "We need to talk, brother." Eli nodded and followed Nate back to the office, Janelle and Renate on their heels.

Chapter 28

Nate sat at his desk. He watched the sun sink below the horizon, then swiveled his chair to face Eli, Janelle, and Renate. "We have a problem."

Renate nodded. "The Arkansas pack has no Alpha."

"Right." Nate frowned. "Koreth tells me that if the wolves start vying for position, it's going to cause problems for all *were* in the state." He leaned forward, elbows on the desk, right hand folded in the left. "I can't be two places at once, but I also can't allow just anyone to step in and take over." He shrugged. "We might have someone as bad or worse than Sinclair or Jackson."

His gaze on Eli's face, Nate waited to let his words sink in. Renate caught on before Eli. She reached for Eli's hand and smiled at her mate when he looked at her. She turned back to face Nate. "What you're suggesting is that Eli and I take on the Alpha responsibilities for the Arkansas pack."

Surprise filled Eli's face. Eli shook his head. "I don't know anything about being Alpha, Nate."

"No, but Renate does, and so does Jabril." Nate sighed. "I won't insist, Eli, but as a Royal..." Nate held up his hand to stop Eli's protests, "...as a made Royal, and Lycos, you are the logical choice."

Eli bit his lip and looked at Renate. "I won't make a decision like this without your input. What do you want to do?"

Renate studied Eli for a moment, then looked at Nate. "May we discuss it and get back to you tomorrow?"

Nate nodded. "It's a life-changing decision." He bowed his head, and muttered, "We've had a lot of those lately." Looking up, he smiled. "Even if you go, why not stay a few weeks, and have a double wedding with us. Mom and Dad would really like to be at both our weddings."

Eli blinked. A silly grin spread across his face, and he turned to look at Renate. "Will you marry me, Renate?"

She laughed. "You can make that decision."

"No, I can't. I won't push you into that without you agreeing." Eli bit his lip. "I'm not much when it comes to being romantic, but..." Ignoring Nate and Janelle, he slipped to his knees before Renate. "Please marry me, Renate."

Renate smiled. "I don't know what to do."

Eli sent a beseeching look to Nate. "Help?"

Nate sent the pleading look to Janelle. "Help?"

Janelle laughed. "I've just about got everything planned. All we need is a second cake and another wedding gown. Oh, and you guys have to get tuxedos. If we're going to do this, we're going to do it right."

Eli turned to Renate, pouted, tilted his head, and gave her sad puppy eyes. "Please?"

Renate started giggling. She grinned at Janelle. "Are they always like this?"

Janelle grinned and nodded. "Always."

Renate smiled at Eli. "Okay. I'll marry you."

Eli whooped Texas style, surged to his feet, picked her up and spun her around. When he stopped, he set her on her feet, then kissed her. "I'll make you happy. I promise."

"You already make me happy, Eli."

Nate laughed. "Why don't you two turn in? Life-changing decisions can wait until tomorrow."

Eli took Renate's hand and pulled her to the door. As he opened the door, Nate cleared his throat. "And Eli." Nate waited until Eli looked back, a question in his eyes.

Nate snickered. "Before you come back to give me your decision, change your trousers. You're gaping."

Chapter 29

After Renate and Eli left for their RV, Nate had Koreth call a meeting of the rest of the Royal Council. He asked Jonathan to bring General Brighton, Secretary Bianchi, Don Dunn, and Phillip Marston to the meeting. Once everyone was seated at the conference table, Nate tapped his palm on the table surface to get their attention. The chatter stopped. Nate swept his gaze over the meeting attendees.

"I called you here to determine how we go forward from here. General, Secretary, this is my Royal Council." As he spoke their names, the men and women of his pack bowed their heads to their visitors. At the confused look on his council's faces, he added, "Eli is also a member of this council, but has been excused from the meeting to discuss the future with his new mate."

Bianchi frowned. "What about the future?"

Nate shrugged. "I have suggested he consider stepping into the Alpha position for the Arkansas pack. When he and Renate make their decision, they will tell you. For now, we will discuss this pack." He glanced at Don and Phillip. "Through no fault or desire of their own, two humans have become aware of my pack."

General Brighton nodded. "Don will return to his duties. Marston will be arrested for his part in kidnapping the Secretary's daughter."

Nate glanced at Marston. The man paled but didn't speak. "Phillip, did you help kidnap Renate?"

"No, Sir."

Nate asked, "What was your part in it?"

"I was brought in as a guard for a dangerous enemy combatant." Marston shrugged. "That's all I knew. She didn't look so dangerous to me. When I realized they weren't feeding her or giving her water, I had to help her. I didn't have time to get her anything to eat, but I did give her water."

Nate nodded. "Renate said you helped her escape. Tell us what happened."

"Yes, Sir. When the shooting started, my partner pulled his pistol and aimed at her. I couldn't let him kill her, so I hit him over the head with the stock of my gun."

"Continue."

"I took the keys from his belt and opened her cell to let her out."

"And when we decided to take you with us?"

"Roger woke up. He called me a traitor and tried to kill me." He swallowed. "That's the first time I ever saw a werewolf. Renate shifted and bit Roger. She pulled him away from me. Then you guys brought me with you."

Nate studied Marston for a minute. "Marston, I'm going to have Koreth, my wolf, verify your statements."

Marston paled and nodded. "I've told the truth."

With a nod, Nate shifted. Koreth pushed into Marston's mind, sifting through his memories. Marston broke into a cold sweat, and his fear stung Koreth's nostrils. A moment later, Koreth shifted back into Nate. Nate nodded. "Koreth deems your statements truthful and complete."

Marston blinked and nodded. His hands gripped the edge of the table. Nate gave him a sympathetic smile. Koreth's mental assault had the man reeling. "The only question now is, what do you want, Marston?"

"Me, Sir?"

"I have several options. Since Koreth and I judge you not guilty..." Nate sent a frown at the general when he opened his mouth to complain. The general's eyes grew wide and he shut his mouth. "I can let you go home. I can give you to the general."

Nate leaned toward him. "Or, I can give you sanctuary here on the ranch. If I let you go home, I can't guarantee the Hunters won't come after you. If the general takes you, you'll end up in a cell somewhere. Maybe for life. If you stay here, you can live and work on the ranch."

"You'd let me stay here?"

"I would. You've proved yourself honest and dependable in battle."

Marston glanced at the general and swallowed. He turned back to Nate. "I don't know much about werewolves, but what I have seen makes me think I would be better off with you." He shrugged. "I want to stay here."

Nate nodded. "Then you are welcome and protected as part of my pack."

Marston's fear spiked.

"I don't expect you to be a werewolf, Phillip, just part of the pack."

The man's fear tapered away. He swallowed and nodded. "I guess I don't really know what that means."

"It means you accept me as your leader, commander, and protector. It means you obey if you are given an order. It means if the pack is attacked, you defend. It means you treat all *were* with respect, and they will in turn respect you."

Nate grinned. "It means we provide you housing, food, and clothes in exchange for whatever type of work you are assigned. The type of work will depend on you. If you like to work with your hands, you can work with the carpenters building and maintaining houses. If you like to garden, we have farm work and yard work. We'll figure out your role later."

For the first time since coming to the ranch, Marston smiled. "I like working with landscaping."

"Good. We have a lot of land that needs it. For now, Phillip, you are dismissed. Meet with Jonathan later this afternoon to figure out your schedule and work details."

"Thank you, Sir." Marston stood. Following the lead of his new packmates, he briefly bowed his head before leaving the room.

When the door closed behind him, Nate looked at the general and raised an eyebrow. "Comments, general?"

"You can't do that, Nate."

"Can't?" Nate sighed and let the wolf light come into his eyes. The slight blue light shimmered around his frame. "I can do that. I did do that. There's nothing you can do about it."

"I have the authority to send in the FBI, Nate. We can close this compound down."

"You won't do that."

"No?"

"No. It would cause a war between human and *were*. Because it would cause war, humans and *were* would die. My charge is to protect both. I will do what's necessary to keep that charge." Nate frowned. "Don't push me, general. You won't like the results."

The general bristled and glared at Nate. Nate's calm gaze seemed to irritate the man even more. He leaned forward. "Look at it this way, general. The U.S. is spared the cost and inconvenience of housing, feeding, and guarding Marston. You don't have to worry about him talking to the wrong person about the wrong things. You don't have to add him to whatever report you have to make on this whole affair. And he won't be in the general population causing problems for *were* and vampires."

Startled, the general stared at Nate. He licked his lips. "Vampires?"

Nate grinned. "I know you're a vampire, general. Don't know much about vampires, but I'm sure you want to stay hidden from the general population as much as *were* do."

Brighton clenched his jaw. A vein in his forehead popped out. After a moment, he forced himself to relax. "Alright, Rollins. You can have him." He leaned forward. "In return, I want a man in your pack."

Nate didn't see that coming. "You want what?"

Brighton took a deep breath and motioned toward Don. "Since you're all so friendly with my corporal, I want him to stay here. As my liaison. I want him to sit in on your 'Royal Council' meetings and report weekly about anything I should know about."

Nate glanced at Don. Don looked uncomfortable but didn't appear to object. Raising his eyebrow at Don, Nate shrugged. "Okay by me. Don, I won't allow the general to order you to do this. This is volunteer only. What do you say?"

Don blinked and looked at the general's frown. "Other than spying, I wouldn't have anything to do." He quirked a lop-sided grin. "Spying wouldn't be so easy, either, since everyone would know that's why I'm here."

Nate laughed. "I like the general's term, liaison, better than spy. As a human, you would be invaluable in my work to keep humans safe from *were*. I already know you would defend the pack if we were attacked."

Don looked at the general. "Never heard of a corporal having liaison duty."

General Brighton frowned. "Under the circumstances, I think a field commission to Second Lieutenant would be appropriate." He looked at Nate. "I want him to have some men under him, though."

Nate frowned. "A liaison I agreed to. An outpost is not acceptable." Nate met the general's glare with one of his own. "Even among vampires, General, I am the Royal Lycos." Relenting, Nate leaned back in his chair. "Tell you what. You have some werewolves in your special unit. You can station two of them here." Nate leaned forward. "Understand, while they are here, they are under my command."

The general sighed. "Very well. I don't like it, though."

A thought occurred to Nate and he looked at Janelle. "How about we give Don our old room? We can refit the office for us, and use the conference room as an office, too?"

A smile lit up Janelle's face, making Nate happy he thought of it. She still had trouble sleeping in their room after Bradley's death, even when Nate was with her. "That's perfect, Nate! Where will we put the other two?"

Dusty leaned forward. "Nate? Since we usually have communal meals, they only need sleeping quarters. They could camp out until Nettie's house is ready, then move into her RV."

Nate nodded. "Perfect. We'll do that." Yawning, he looked at Janelle. "Sweetheart, would you have someone make us some coffee?"

Janelle nodded. Rather than call someone, she walked

to the sink in the side counter and fixed it herself. While she worked on the coffee, Nate turned to Bianchi.

"Secretary, Janelle and I are having a wedding in about two weeks. We've asked Eli and Renate to join us in a double-wedding, so that my foster-parents, Eli's mom and dad, can attend. They have agreed. You are welcome to stay here until then, or if you need to return to Washington, you can come back. Up to you."

Nate nearly laughed at the delight filling Bianchi's face. "I need to get to Washington for a few days, but I wouldn't miss it." He frowned. "Nate, if I don't extend invitations to the President and some of his staff, it's going to look a bit strange."

"Invite them. Just let me know if you have to set up any special security. We'll work with you on it, but I want you or the general to be in charge. A wedding is not a good time for a *were*/human incident."

Bianchi nodded, concern on his face. "I'll think of something."

"Good. Janelle will make sure you have the details you need. We won't have room for everyone who attends to stay, but if it's not too late, I'll reserve a block of rooms at a hotel in Hallettsville."

Janelle sat beside Nate. Coffee began perking in the large urn. "It's already taken care of, Nate. I rented all the rooms in the Texas Bay Inn for the entire month of June. I wasn't sure when the wedding would be and wanted to make sure we had it for the right dates."

Don grinned. "When you guys do something, you don't do it by half measures."

Nate grinned at Don, then smiled at Janelle. "That's perfect. Set a date, yet?"

“June 2nd?” She put her hand on her baby bump.

Nate looked at her and realized the baby had grown since yesterday. “When are you due?’

“June 14th.” She laughed. “It’s okay, Nate. There’s no way we could pull all the strings together any sooner.”

Nate took a deep breath, then reached for her hand. “June 2nd it is, then.” He raised her hand and kissed her fingers.

*****

After they retired to their room, while Janelle showered Nate sat on the bed and stared at the wall. He was forgetting something. It irritated. Standing up, he walked the floor, then sat in the wing chair in the corner. His thumb drummed on his thigh. He shook his head and rolled his neck. His gaze landed on Janelle’s school laptop sitting on the dresser.

Jumping to his feet, he barged into the bathroom. Janelle had just stepped out of the shower and had a towel wrapped around her. Nate pulled her into his arms. “When do you graduate?”

She laughed at him. “All my work will be turned in by Friday. Next week is exam week. Why?” She suddenly frowned and caught his biceps in her hands. “Nate, I have to go to San Antonio every day next week for the exams.”

“I’ll go with you.”

“You have so much to do!”

“I’m Alpha. I’ll assign someone else to do everything. You can’t go to San Antonio alone so close to your delivery date.”

“Are you sure?”

"If you don't go, you won't graduate?"

She nodded. "That's right. No exams, no graduation."

"Then it's settled. Get me the schedule for your exams. I'll drive you, and we can spend some time alone while we're there. If you want to, we'll even rent a hotel room for a few days and just stay there." Nate kissed her. "You've worked too hard for this, not to see it through."

"Thank you, Nate."

He brushed her damp hair off her forehead. "Do you want to walk?"

"No."

"Are you sure?"

"The graduation ceremony is on June 1, Nate. I don't have time for a graduation and a wedding. I prefer the wedding. Besides, it's just pomp and circumstance. I'll have the degree, even if I don't walk."

"We can make it work if you want both."

Janelle shook her head and smiled. "No. Have I told you today that I love you?"

Nate pretended to think about it. "Not sure. Guess you'll have to say it again."

Janelle giggled. "I love you, Nate Rollins."

"And I love you, future Mrs. Nate Rollins."

Chapter 30

Nate slipped into his tuxedo jacket and turned to look at himself in the full-length mirror Janelle insisted he hang on the back of the door in their new bedroom. It fit as well as the tailor promised it would. He and Eli hadn't been able to find tuxes to rent in their size. As a last resort, he commissioned a tailor to make them. With such a short lead time, the commission was exorbitant, but he thought Janelle would be happy with the results.

Turning, he grinned at his brother, who wore a matching tux. "You clean up pretty good."

"So do you." Eli grinned. "Wonder if Mom and Dad are here, yet."

"I don't know. Janelle really wanted them here for the rehearsal dinner last night. She was so disappointed when Dad couldn't get off early enough to drive down."

A tap sounded at the door, Nate turned. "Come in."

When his mom's head popped in, he and Eli both rushed to her, grabbing her in a three-way hug. Nate leaned back and whistled at the blue chiffon gown his mother wore. "Mom, you're gorgeous!"

Nate blinked when she actually giggled. Behind her, their dad cleared his throat. "Leaving me to stand in the hall, boys?"

Nate gently pulled his mom into the room, giving his dad room to walk in. Wearing his dress uniform, the Major smiled at his sons. "Someone finally got you two in tuxes."

Nate grinned. "Took some doing, but we finally convinced Eli he had to wear it."

Eli shoulder bumped Nate. "Was you that needed

convincing."

Major Curtis Thomas looked from one to the other and grinned. "I suspect it took some fancy talking for both of you."

Cynthia Thomas laughed. "Unless these ladies of yours have you wrapped around their little fingers. Which is it?"

When Nate and Eli exchanged sheepish grins, she laughed again. "I thought that might be the way of it. I can't wait to meet the girls my boys care so much for."

The Major grinned, then his face became more serious. "Nate, there's something I have to ask you." He nodded at their mother. "I've been given permission to speak in front of your mom."

Nate took in his mother's surprise and looked at his dad. "What's up?"

"General Brighton offered me a billet here on the ranch. He suggested there was some reason for needing a military presence here."

Nate cut his gaze to Eli. Eli shrugged. "It's your ranch. I'm headed to Arkansas next week."

"Marshal Eli Thomas! Arkansas?" Cynthia pouted. "So soon?"

Eli gave her a quick hug. "Sorry, Mom. I have to get to work."

She sighed and nodded. "You military men are always on the go. I thought you worked in San Antonio, now."

"I have a new job. I'm, uh, well, it's kind of hard to explain."

Nate laughed. "He's the ramrod of a place out there."

"What company?"

"Um, we call it the Ozark Pack."

Eli gave him a severe frown and rolled his eyes. Nate

just grinned. "He's going to be head of the company, fixing the mistakes the former CEO made, almost driving the company to ruin."

"Oh." She smiled. "You should be able to handle that."

"Of course, Mom." Eli gave her shoulders a squeeze.

The major cleared his throat again and raised an eyebrow. "Nate?"

Nate sucked air between his teeth. Cynthia huffed. She never did like that habit. He gave his mother an apologetic look. "Sorry, Mom." He turned to his dad. "You are welcome here, Sir. There's a lot that might...surprise you, but you are always welcome on my ranch."

"My ranch? You both said that. How did you ever afford this place? Police officers, even detectives, don't make that kind of money. Not even with your retirement from the Marines."

"I guess you could say I'm marrying into it."

"Oh, Nate!" The distress in Cynthia's voice made Nate feel like cringing.

"No, Mom. It's not like that. I didn't really want it, but it comes with the territory. If I marry Janelle, the ranch is mine. It's in her brother's will." Nate grinned. "It's a pretty big responsibility."

"And the need for a military presence?"

Nate looked at his father. The man always did hone in on the basics. "Can we talk about this tomorrow? I don't want to, uh, cause any issues before the wedding."

"No." His mom's firm answer startled Nate. "If there are issues, we need to know before the wedding."

Nate bit his lip. When his dad nodded agreement, Nate sighed. He looked at Eli. "How do you suggest we do this?"

"Your call. You're the boss."

"The boss?" Cynthia looked totally confused. They had argued over who was 'boss' for years. "Nate, Eli, what's going on here?"

The brothers exchanged glances, then Nate took his mother's hand and pulled her to the bed. "Sit down, and I'll try to explain." He looked at the major. "Sir, if you'll sit with her? This might upset her, and I think she'll be more comfortable if you're with her."

Frowning, Curtis sat beside his wife. She clasped the major's hand with both hers. "Nate? You're scaring me."

"That's something I wouldn't willingly do, Mom. I will never, ever hurt you. You have to know that."

At his insistence, she nodded. "I know."

"Okay." Nate took two steps away from his parents and looked at Eli. "They may need your...help. You don't...uh, just...don't."

Eli nodded and sat on the other side of his mom. "Mother, when you see what Nate's going to do, understand that it's okay. He and I are both okay."

Cynthia searched Eli's face for reassurance, then nodded. "Okay?"

Eli swallowed and nodded at Nate. "Just be careful not to damage the tux, will you? Janelle will kill you."

Nate gave him a sickly grin and swallowed. When he shifted, his mother's eyes grew huge and froze open. She stopped breathing. Koreth whined and looked at Eli. Eli put his arm behind his mother and rubbed her back. "Breathe, Mom. It's okay. It's just Nate. He won't hurt you."

She caught a ragged breath and swallowed, then turned her face to her husband. "Did you know?"

His gaze still on Nate, expression tightly controlled, Curtis shook his head. Nate shifted into a human. He turned to inspect his tux for damage, relieved when he found none.

"Nate?"

Nate looked at his dad. "Sir?"

"How...I mean, when…? What happened?"

Nate pulled the only chair in the room closer and sat down. "My real parents died when I was a kid. You know that."

His parents glanced uncertainly at each other, then nodded at Nate. "Well, they were werewolves. Only I didn't know it." Nate unbuttoned his shirt and pulled out the medallion. "Have you ever seen this?"

"Seen what?"

Nate sighed. "Koreth, can you help them see it?" He felt Koreth's affirmative.

His mother looked behind her, then looked back at Nate. "Who are you talking to?"

"Koreth is my wolf. You just saw him." He held up the medallion again. "Do you see this now?"

His parents looked at his hand, then both startled as a bronze medallion suddenly shimmered into sight. "What's that?" asked his dad.

"My father gave me this before he died. He told me it's a family heirloom. I was required to always wear it. I always have." Nate looked from his mom to his dad. "The medallion is charmed. Humans can't see it, and other werewolves can't sense me when I'm wearing it. My dad gave it to me for protection. A powerful werewolf wanted to kill me."

His mother gasped. "Nate!"

"It's okay. He's dead, now, so I'm safe." Giving his parents a minute to digest what he told them, he looked at

Eli and raised his eyebrow.

After an almost undetectable hesitation, Eli nodded. "We might as well."

"Might as well what?" His dad's voice was strained. "There's more?"

The brothers exchanged worried looks, then Nate nodded. "When we were about thirteen, we got in trouble for cutting our hands to be blood-brothers. Remember?"

"So?" Suddenly, the major's eyes took on a shocked expression. "In the stories, if a werewolf bites a human..."

"Well, that's not quite correct. Bites only make a human into a werewolf if there is an exchange of blood."

"An exchange of blood?" Cynthia's face paled. "Your blood-brother ceremony?"

Eli stood up and moved to stand beside Nate's chair. He shimmered into Jabril, whined at his parents, then shimmered back. "Nate didn't know he was a werewolf, then. The medallion kept him from being able to shift. He didn't find out until last March. We think that since his blood transformed me into a werewolf changeling, and made me his true blood-brother, the medallion prevented me from shifting, too."

"Oh, my." Cynthia lifted a trembling hand to wipe the single tear that tracked her cheek. "Are you okay, Eli?"

"I'm fine, Mom. In fact, as a werewolf, I'm pretty much indestructible. Very little can hurt me."

The major ran his fingers through his hair. Nate almost smiled at the mess his dad made of his perfectly combed head. He swallowed. "What's this have to do with the wedding?"

Nate let Eli answer this one. "The girls we are marrying are werewolves, too. Nate is the pack Alpha. He's in charge of everything that happens here. I'll be heading to Arkansas to take over the Ozark Pack. Their Alpha recently died, and someone needs to step in to maintain peace."

"The Ozark Pack." Cynthia tilted her head and shot a reproving look at Nate. "Nate, how could you?"

"Sorry, Mom. It's kind of hard to explain without going into a lot of, well, for want of a better term, explanations."

Curtis leaned forward. "So why does the general think there needs to be a military presence here?"

"He doesn't quite trust me not to let the werewolves cause trouble. The man I mentioned? The one trying to kill me? He came here and challenged me. By *were* law, I had to fight him. He died. Eli will be taking over his pack."

Cynthia released her husband's hand. She stood and walked to the brothers. Bending over, she gave Nate a hug, then turned and gave Eli a hug, too. "I don't care what you are. You're still my sons."

Nate grinned at Cynthia, then looked at Curtis. "And you, Sir? You're the only dad I had growing up. I don't want to lose you."

Curtis huffed. "Guess I'll be accepting that billet." He looked Nate in the eye. "If anyone is keeping an eye on my sons, I'm going to keep an eye on him."

Nate grinned. "There is one more thing."

Cynthia frowned. "Is it as startling as werewolves?"

"No. At least, I hope not." When Eli snickered, Nate glared at him, then said in a rush. "Janelle and I are having a baby in about two weeks."

Chapter 31

Dottie looked up from brushing her youngest daughter's hair and laughed. "What happened to your hair, Ben?"

Ben stepped off the bottom step of the staircase, reached up and touched his bald head, and the strip of gray hair curving around the back of his head. Rueful, he shrugged. "Nate insisted on inviting guys from the precinct to the wedding. Last time they saw me, I looked this way." He pursed his lips when Marsha and Sissy giggled.

"That's enough, girls." Dottie scowled at her daughters. "Ben looks very dignified."

The two girls, one a young teen, the other six-years-old, caught their lips in their teeth to stop their giggles, but humor danced in their eyes. After an exaggerated look of hurt, Ben grinned at them and winked. "It does look kind of silly, doesn't it?"

They both giggled again. Marsha grabbed Sissy's hand. "Let's go tell everyone, so they can get over laughing before the wedding starts."

Ben laughed at the reproving look Dottie sent the girls as they ran out of the room. "You really think I look dignified?"

She grinned. "I do."

"Thank you, ma'am!"

Dottie ducked her head, but not before Ben saw the telltale glow that climbed her neck and suffused her face. "I have to go help with the refreshments." Dottie followed her girls out the front door.

Ben chuckled and shook his head. He stroked his

freshly-shaved chin with his thumb and forefinger, then raised an eyebrow. "I think she likes us, Marcel."

His panther purred.

*****

The first story of the gazebo was decorated with billows of white chiffon, pulled up at each of the eight posts, and anchored with a bouquet of pink and lilac roses. In the center of the gazebo floor, two tables held two massive, gorgeously decorated tiered wedding cakes, one with pink roses, the other with lilac roses.

Between the two tables, a third table held a massive crystal punch bowl filled with pink punch. Nate swept his gaze over the decorations and felt a grin tug at his lips. Two sections of chairs lined up on either side of the wide aisle that led to the gazebo steps. A long carpet runner ran from the back row of chairs to the steps. Rose petals, also pink and lilac, lined the carpet. Nate's grin grew into a big smile. The ladies did a great job getting everything set up.

At such short notice, the president's and vice-president's families had not been able to make the wedding. To Nate's knowledge, no one was disappointed. Not even Bianchi. It definitely made the security issue easier to deal with.

The smell of barbecue for the wedding dinner wafted from the picnic shelter. Dusty and Jonathan put the briskets on to smoke twelve hours ago. The beef should be nice and tender by now.

When the orchestra Janelle hired started playing the Wedding March, Nate heard the wedding guests stand. He turned to face the aisle created between the guest's chairs.

Dressed in a pink gown with lilac roses, Flora walked, Will at her side, down the aisle. They slowly walked up the steps to the top floor of the gazebo, then split and walked to stand one on either side of Dusty. Laying on the floor in front of Dusty, tongue hanging out, Tig ignored the large pink and purple bow the teen girls tied around his neck.

Anxious not to miss Janelle's entrance, Nate didn't turn to watch them climb the steps. When Janelle and Renate appeared at the end of the aisle, Nate caught his breath. Janelle and Renate walked side-by-side to their grooms where they waited at the bottom of the gazebo stairs.

Nate's gaze never left Janelle as she slowly walked to him. He smiled. Her empire waisted gown camouflaged her pregnant tummy in multiple layers of lace. Nate took Janelle's hand, tucked it into his arm, then slowly walked up the stairs to the center of the two-story gazebo where Dusty waited to officiate the service.

Behind them, he heard Eli and Renate walk up the steps. Nate and Janelle moved to the left, giving Eli and Renate room to stand on their right. The music stopped and their guests' clothing rustled as they sat down.

He winked at Janelle and turned to look at Dusty. Dusty cleared his throat. "Welcome to the first Texas Ranch wedding. We are gathered..."

Nate glanced at Janelle. *She's so beautiful!* The tears on her face caught his attention. *Mine!* Nate grinned at Koreth's happy declaration. Lost in her eyes, he had to be prodded when it was his turn to say, "I do." Nate smiled and added, "Forever and for always."

Janelle's brilliant smile warmed him all the way to his toes. A moment later, she nodded. "I do. Forever and for always." Never taking his gaze off Janelle's eyes, Nate waited while Eli and Renate made their vows.

Dusty finished the service. "I now pronounce you husband and wife. You may kiss your brides."

Reese and Adrian started cheering when Nate lifted her bridal veil and captured Janelle's lips in a long, deep, romantic kiss. He assumed Eli was doing the same with Renate but didn't look up to check. The rest of the wolves and panthers joined the cheering. Part of Nate noticed the cheers, and was relieved they didn't howl, yowl, and growl. Some of their guests might have been startled.

Leaning back, he gave Janelle a soft smile. "I love you."

"I love you, too, Nate. Forever and for always."

The next book in the series is Wolf's Huntsman.

Thank You!

Thank you for reading, *Wolf's Mission*, the third book in the Texas Ranch Wolf Pack series.

Please Leave a Review

Reviews are the lifeblood of books in today's market. If you read this book, please take the time to leave an honest review.

Reviews are not book reports. They are just a few words to let other readers know how you liked or didn't like the book.

Authors, especially indie authors, depend on reviews to help readers find their books. Good or bad reviews help an author on the journey as an author.

You can also find Lynn Nodima's books and stories at:

www.lynnnodima.com

Lynn's Books

The Texas Ranch Wolf Pack Series

Wolf's Man
Wolf's Claim
Wolf's Mission
Wolf's Huntsman
Wolf's Trust
Wolf's Reign
Wolf's Queen
Wolf's Enemy
Wolf's Rage
Wolf's Quest
Wolf's Guard
Wolf's Duty

Texas Ranch Wolf Pack World

Wolf's Sorrow
Wolf's Mate
Wolf's Heart
Wolf's Dragon
Wolf's Princess
Wolf's Son

Texas Ranch Wolf Pack Box Sets

Wolf's Destiny: Books 1-6
Wolf's Victory: Books 7-12